Till I Come Marching Home

A World War II Romance

Elsan H. Stafford

Stafford, Elsan H.
ISBN: 9-798416480431
Till I Come Marching Home / Elsan H. Stafford – 1st
ed.

Printed in the USA

TABLE OF CONTENTS

DEDICATION

To the two dearest people in my life and most enthusiastic supporters... albeit my sternest critics, namely: my son, Patrick and his lovely wife, Liane, I hereby dedicate this, my most recent contribution to the medium of belles letters. Through their unselfish devotion and inexhaustible assistance, the success of my labor of love has been made possible.

PROLOGUE

He sat there at the small table on the sidewalk cafe, a stone's throw from the blue waters of the sultry Mediterranean. The strand that lay between was thronged to the inch with the usual mass of Sunday bathers. The cacophonous infusion of their myriad voices into the intermittent roar of the waves that crashed against the crags along the shore, tainted the summer air. But the young man seemed oblivious to the distraction of the concomitant tumult.

To a casual observer, the slight upward tilt of his head suggested the focus of his gaze was directed further out to sea, where in the distance, gracing the pictorial seascape, a painted vessel lay quietly at anchor, its white sails furled and lashed, its highest mast bearing a flag that proudly waved in the gentle breeze... a star spangled banner! Rather, it was the anticipatory posture of a man in the strained attitude of listening for some particular sound out of the mysterious past illusive of its capture.

The extravagance of all the artistic beauty of this scenery was wasted on the visual senses of the silent erstwhile observer. The large, dark glasses he wore to protect his eyes from the bright summer sun, and the red and white cane he couched across his lap attested to an affliction of extreme visual disability. Beneath the recent tan of his handsome features, acquired from the long sea voyage from America, lurked a pallor suggestive of a protracted and exacerbating illness, both physical and mental. On his forehead, just above his left eyebrow, he bore a six-inch livid scar... a remnant of his military service with the Second U.S. Infantry Division on its drive from the bloody beach at Normandy to Paris and beyond, which a bursting shell fragment had ended abruptly several months before the capture of Berlin and the cessation of hostilities in the European theater of World War Two. His wound had assessed a double indemnity, for with his sight, imposing fate had also deprived him of his memory!

At the same table, across from him, sat his constant companion and manservant, as well as physician; an older man who had attended him the several years he had been hospitalized, and subsequently retained by him upon his discharge from the military hospital in New York. Three more years had elapsed since then... years lost in time, whose ravages were inconsequential to him, for time has no dimension to a man who lies inert in darkness and is bereft of the knowledge of identity. A vegetable has no knowledge of self!

Some time before leaving America on his voyage to France, his functional memory suddenly began resurrecting itself. His mind became spasmodically assailed with intermittent and increasingly vivid flashes of disturbing, nostalgic scenes and sounds, attended each time by a precursor of intense physical pain in his head. Finally, as these transient images persisted their replication and extended their tenure of existence in his mind, he gradually began to discriminate their structure. Then, with seemingly sentient determination, they metamorphosed finally into some semblance of availability he could relate to, and realized they must somehow have been a consequential, if not vital link in the broken chain of his interrupted life!

Yes, he knew he was alive now! He knew he was a man! It was the eternal darkness he did not understand! But instinctively he knew these pictorial flashes were a psychic or spiritual message importuning him to reclaim an essence of great value that had once belonged to him and, still existing, could be his again, for the taking.

Progressively with each resurgent experience the accompanying physical pain diminished, to be superseded by a nostalgic echo in his empty heart, and an escalating resolve to recapture his memory and secure the substance of this lost beauty that seemed so dear to him.

And then one day, as he reclined fretfully in his easy chair listening as his friend read to him from a book of poetry, a vital incident of memory flooded back upon him for an instant, in a great deluge of passion and alarm! And at last he knew his pain was love, for these two are inseparable. And he knew that love was stronger than death and that love had given back his life to him. If only a thread! It was a clue... a beginning! Yes, there had been a girl. And they had been inconsolably in love!

He held the reins of his life in his grasp once more, and he knew what he must do. With unrestrained eagerness he interrupted the reader, almost shouting: "Richards! I remember... I have seen. I must go to her. Come, let us begin at once, now... Prepare to leave for France. It is there I will find her... My beautiful Mignonette." He paused for a moment, struggling for rationality. "Dear God!" he groaned, "How long has it been? Years? Oh, my darling. What must she think of me." Again, "Tell me, how long has it been?" His voice was distraught with anguish.

His companion, himself shaken by his friend's exhibition of unrestrained grief and his revelation of memory, answered in a tone adopted to soothe the young man's dismay, but his words were also designed to impart the necessary and inescapable truth. "More than five years, I'm afraid, Colonel, since you received your wound..." He paused, then continued, directing his speech to the matter of the moment, "Your yacht is ready to sail, sir. I have arranged for you to meet with a number of brain specialists in Europe, who have indicated optimistic hope your sight and your complete memory can be restored. We can leave by tomorrow evening, if you wish. It's early summer, and the weather is calm. I'll alert the crew at once, to make ready."

"My wound? Yes, of course! There must have been a wound. That explains much of this." He paused thoughtfully, "And this darkness... I am blind!" And then hopefully, "But my memory... it is returning. I must be patient. And I must find my Mignonette. I must find her. I will do whatever I must to accomplish that... and as quickly as possible." He reached out and touched Richards, his voice tinged with restrained emotion... "You have been a great friend to me, sir. I shall be ever obliged to you."

CHAPTER ONE
The Meeting

Captain Kilmeade sat at his desk in the large pyramidal field tent, holding in his hand an official communication he had received earlier that morning from the Allied High Command. He had read it carefully several times before, and each time, a smile of pride and satisfaction slowly crept across his tired and careworn features in tacit response to the message it contained. Paris had fallen to the advancing allied troops two weeks earlier, and the German army was in stubborn retreat toward Berlin. Delinquent paper work was slowly catching up with individual military personnel matters.

As he sat there musing over the dramatic incidents of the last seven traumatic months a young man about his own age pushed open the canvas flap that covered the tent entrance and approached him in a respectful military manner. He touched his hand to his brow, executing and maintaining an austere salute as he stood at attention.

Kilmeade returned his salute. "At ease, Sergeant. There's no formality between you and me when we're alone. You know that."

"Thank you, Major Kilmeade, sir. But this occasion is worthy of special treatment... if you will allow me." He paused, a smile of affection and deep appreciation forming across his sunburnt face. "I would like to be the first to congratulate you on your long overdue and well deserved promotion, and," he added, "for the two Silver Stars you are now going to receive. Sergeant Bowen and Corporal Richards will be especially appreciative, knowing that saving their lives was worth the decorations." He paused, then continued, "Our men are ready, sir, and the awarding delegation is assembled and waiting." He paused again and grinned broadly, "If I may say so, sir, old `Fart and Fall Back' Colonel Wide Bottom is in charge of the ceremonies. Nothing's ever perfect these days."

Kilmeade laughed. "Man, you got that right! Let's go then, and get it over with. Walk out with me, Sergeant Tulloch. I need your support... and get those two rockers on your sleeve, that I put you in for, months ago. I'm not the only damned hero around here!" They strode out through the tent opening together, walking in step and shoulder to shoulder toward the large assemblage of troops in the near distance. These two warriors were an inseparable unit! The catalysis of war forges a cohesive union between like elements of human aspiration, such as courage and love!

* * *

Paris at night at this interval of the war, was thronged with conflict-weary military personnel and grateful, rejoicing citizens. The City of Lights had become the mecca of forgetfulness for the former, and rejuvenated hope for the latter! The Allied rescue effort had driven the invaders some forty miles safely beyond the border of the long- beleaguered city, and ultimate victory was now accepted as imminent reality. The final chapter of the great war was being written in the headquarters of the Allied High Command!

In the midst of this revelry Major Kilmeade sat at a table in jovial conversation with a number of fellow officers from his battalion. The nightclub was filled

6

with merriment and laughter. All U. S. military personnel were decked out in formal uniform... the order of the day for those on public recreation. The overtly handsome appearance of Major Kilmeade was resplendently embellished with his newly acquired oak-leaf insignia of rank, and his gallant medallion with two silver stars. The forager, a braided purple cord worn encircling the recipient's arm and shoulder, added further grace to his splendor. All of his battalion had been awarded this same distinction of valor.

A stage situated at the far end of the large establishment was occupied by a small orchestra playing instrumental music that was popular in that era. Suddenly a fanfaronade of music burst out, and a bright spotlight illumined the stage. Standing, draped in its brilliant flood, poised the most beautiful woman the Major had ever seen! The predominately masculine crowd roared its approval. Kilmeade sat in silence, entranced! And then, as the exuberant greeting receded, she began to sing!

Her first song, rendered in obeisance to the United States, was "God Bless America." She sang the words in brave and difficult English. The applause was deafening! She performed a number of additional songs, mostly in French, and then the orchestra broke for refreshments, attending at the large and elegant liquor bar some little distance from where the major was seated.

A compelling and irresistible impulse seized Kilmeade, and he arose and strode to where the vocalist sat alone sipping a popular French cordial. "Mademoiselle," he began, somewhat uncertainly, "May I express my appreciation for the pleasure your songs have given me, and the remarkable beauty of your voice. And may I also respectfully take the liberty of introducing myself? I am Major Scott Kilmeade, Headquarters, 1st Regiment, 2nd Division, A.E.F., and your most humble servant." He smiled, almost shyly, and bowed in diffidence. Major Kilmeade was not what could be termed a lady's man, and was a bit out of his usual character in the presence of a beautiful woman who stirred his emotions. Such things as classical music, sunset, a rainbow, or anything of extreme beauty too esoteric to be readily comprehended, had a way of humbling him.

The girl blushed prettily, her beautiful blue eyes devouring the handsome officer. She arose in greeting. "Merci, monsieur! You are most kind to speak so nice. And I am called Mignonette." She returned his bow with a pretty curtsey.

"Will you sing again tonight? I must hear you sing another song before I go," he said, hopefully. "A special song that I can take with me."

"Oui, monsieur, I will sing just for you. What is this special song you wish to hear?"

"Great," he replied eagerly. "Do you know the American song, 'Don't Sit Under The Apple Tree With Anyone Else But Me'? It is a favorite of mine."

She smiled coquettishly, "Oui, monsieur, I know it well. It is also one of mine."

He looked at her levelly, then. "This is all so very sweet of you," he said. "I will listen for our song, and then I must go. I will only say, au revoir, now, for I will most certainly see you again." With a twinkle in his eye, he smiled and bowed and strode away... an inexplicable and buoyant feeling of something like hope in his heart. It had been years since anything but despair had claimed his thoughts for any future in his life. Living so long in the presence of violence and sudden death would do that to a man. He had seen too many men die to believe he would survive. At the beginning, on the beach at Normandy, he had been but a second lieutenant. Then slowly and inexorably, as each officer in his company was killed on the long and bloody trek eastward, he rose in rank to fill that vacancy, finally taking command of his company, and then becoming executive officer of the battalion.

Her eyes followed him as he walked away, her thoughts also much the same as his, for she had lived even longer with death. Did she dare entertain this remote thing called hope? But hope is eternal, and from what she was suddenly feeling now, life seemed real again!

And so, she sang again... the song he loved! And many of her friends later said it was the best performance she had ever given. And her heart smiled, for it knew the truth of why it was: He would come to her again. His eyes had told her so! And he knew he must come, and that she would be waiting, for love speaks a promise that flies on the wings of a song.

The following days were busy ones for the Allies. The final and decisive attack was soon to be launched, that would crush the reeling enemy and bring an end to the greatest armed conflict ever fought. The army of the Axis was being temporarily contained at its home border while fresh personnel and supplies were rushed to the front lines to support the Allied offensive.

From daylight till dusk each day, Kilmeade worked tirelessly with his men to prepare for the enormous task that confronted them. But his attitude had changed dramatically. His labor now was tempered with hope and optimism and a rejuvenated eagerness for life, for his evenings were spent in the idyllic company of someone who had restored him into the province of happiness and the stirred belief that there might be a realistic future to enjoy. One thing he knew: he would feast his pleasure on the bounty of the present, and let the future take care of itself. It has often been said that a happiness shared is twice as enjoyable; but love cannot be altered by mathematic formula. The magnitude of its sweetness flourishes in the realm of infinity, and answers only to the constituent largesse of the lovers' souls!

The nightclub where they met each night soon became the most talked about entertainment spot in Paris. The French are notorious for their appreciation of romance, and Kilmeade and Mignonette made no effort to conceal their mutual affection. Time was too short, too pressing for both of them, and their emotions too intense to observe any mundane amenities attending a conventional love affair. When love speaks, its voice commands. Without choice of avenue, one must but obey.

If he ever knew they were the cynosure of sympathetic and admiring attention, he paid no heed, for his position of rank precluded any frivolity among the military personnel. As for the opinion of the French citizenry, they were beneath the scope of his consideration. They in turn were in awe of him, for he was an imposing model of the austere and conquering American military machine, as well as personifying their concept of a liberating hero.

Several nights after their initial acquaintance he made arrangement to meet her the next afternoon and she would escort him around the city to visit some of the interesting spots he had read of, and was anxious to see.

His jeep driver parked them in front of the nightclub where she worked and picked her up when she came along. From there they drove to the Montmartre district of Paris and stopped at a sidewalk cafe, where he dismissed the driver, with instructions to return and pick them up in two hours. "You're on your own till then, Corporal. Stay out of trouble." He looked at his watch. The noncom did likewise.

A waiter appeared, and they ordered wine. "Garcon, will you request your combo to play a special song for my lady friend and me?" He took a bill from his wallet and extended it to the man as he spoke.

"Yes, monsieur, I will be most happy to do so, but..." he shook his head, "no money, Major. All of Paris knows who you are. And the song, it is, 'Don't sit under the...' how you say, 'apple tree,' n'est pas?"

"Oui, c'est vrai."

He left quickly, and soon returned with their order, just as the first strains of their song came to them. "Your wine, monsieur... and your chanson! Please enjoy." He bowed and left.

The two sweethearts sipped their drink in ecstatic silence as they listened, each one's eyes caressing the face of the other... each heart filled with the sublime passion they felt and wished to share! As they listened a great feeling of trust came to them.

The last nostalgic notes of the song died away, and Kilmeade hastily scribbled a note on a paper napkin, took out a few bills, folded them together and tucked them under his half-empty wine glass. "Shall we stroll around a bit?"

As he started to rise, the orchestra struck up a reprise of their song, and he resumed his seat, smiling. "Your

Frenchies are sure a romantic lot. God bless 'em!" And then, thoughtfully, "I suppose some of it is gratitude . . .and appreciation for what we Americans have suffered in their behalf. You are a great people! We have never forgotten what your Lafayette did for us a hundred and fifty years ago. And we never will."

Mignonette's responsive smile, and the moisture in her eyes, bespoke the emotion his words evoked. "My gallant American!" she cried. You are America's Marechal Ney... The bravest of the brave!"

"And you, my dearest one, are like none other I have ever known," he murmured softly. "You are the fairest of the fair!"

She blushed her appreciation at the effusive compliment, but its oblique reference to any special esteem or affection he held for her gave her pause for a sobering thought that had been of consideration to her for some time, and which she now felt must be resolved, for both of them. She was beginning to care too much. She must know his true intentions! "This favorite song of yours, about the apple tree, I mean. Does it have... that is... I mean to say..." She paused, at a loss for the proper words. The question had at first seemed simple enough to ask, and she believed she had a right to know the answer. But she cringed now at its patent boldness and its suggestion of a commitment on her part that might be too presumptuous or prematurely affirmed. Her face was crimson!

His interrupting soft words of reassurance, and understanding smile eased her embarrassment. "No," he said, "there's no such girl back home, no sweetheart waiting for me. The sentiment of the song just appeals to me. I have often thought it would be great if I had someone waiting for me when this terrible war is over, and I could pick up with my life again and have someone beautiful and loving to share it with. When I hear that song it gives me back a little of the hope I lost on Omaha Beach so long ago. And then, when I saw you the other night, and you sang my song for me, I knew it could be possible again to reclaim my life and its dream!" He looked at her with resuscitated hope in his eyes. "Can you be that girl! Will you wait for me, alone, under the apple tree?"

And there it was! He had made the necessary commitment that properly the man should make to establish an honest understanding in any relationship of an emotional or romantic nature. His unselfish consideration of her tenuous position was nonpareil, as was her gratitude for it.

Her responding tears were like stars in her eyes as the reply from her heart rushed close upon his question, "Oui, oui vraiment! I am that girl! I shall be there when you come to me! And I shall sing our song each day until you come!" Smiling, she added, "If this war should never end, and you do not come, I will be there still... waiting! There will be no other love for me! And I shall live, and haply die, beneath the blessing of our trysting tree."

The bit of melodramatic dialogue at the end of her speech did not diminish the emphasis and sincerity of the initial part of her impassioned answer on Kilmeade, but was appended as persuasion to lighten the unguarded, naive extravagance of her initial fervor she had sincerely felt. But it too, was spoken from her heart!

With equal sincerity he replied, "Rest your faith on the words of a man of profound honor, and who is as profoundly in love! If I live, and am able, I will surely come!" And then in empathy to any possible imposition her forthright display of honest emotion may have caused her, he added, "Scott `Able' Kilmeade, they call me... at your service, Mademoiselle." His soft laugh revealed the innocuity of his humor.

They strolled about for a while then, holding hands, their first physical gesture of intimacy. Walking side by side only frustrated their desire for closeness. They had to touch! The unpredictable and tenuous future confronting them imposed the desperate aspect of a pressing urgency to their relationship. It was a tacit mood, spoken by neither, but shared by both.

Their walk brought them at length before a large building that served as a music hall, and out from which emanated the orchestral strains of a major classical symphony. He stopped and turned to her. "Do you like instrumental music," he asked.

"Yes, I like all beautiful music," she answered. "But I am partial to the popular modern love songs." She looked up at him and smiled, a twinkle in her eye. "I prefer music with words, so I can sing them to you."

His soft laugh bespoke his pleasure from her revelation. "You have a beautiful voice. And I love to hear you sing," he quickly added. "But I must point out that some of the most stirring music ever composed is strictly instrumental. For instance, that music you are hearing now is a great classic. It is the Andante Cantabile of Tchaikovsky's Fifth Symphony." He paused, and then continued thoughtfully but without boast, "And the "A" string on one of the second violins is flat. It needs to be tightened."

She looked at him disbelievingly. "You know that just by listening?" She shook her head in wonder. "How can you do that?"

"I don't really know," he replied matter-of-factly. "A gift, I guess. Beethoven and Liszt could do it... and a few others, I suppose. But I'm no musician." He shrugged, "It's like anything else you naturally have and just take for granted. It has been useful to me, though." His voice took on a sober tone, "For instance, I can accurately calculate the distance and location of the enemy by listening to the sound of their gunfire. It was your Napoleon who coined the phrase, `Always march to the sound of the guns!' Marechal Grouchy ignored that stipulation during Napoleon's engagement with the Duke of Wellington at Waterloo. And the consequence of that blunder is indelibly written in history! One's sense of sound is sometimes more important than sight. No one can see around a corner, or over the distance span of ten miles."

He smiled good-naturedly at her manifestation of naive amazement, then continued with his enlightening revelations, enjoying her sincerity of acknowledgement and belief. "A moment ago I detected a rumble of thunder over that way," pointing toward the east. "About fifteen miles from here. We will likely have a rain shower shortly. We'd best be getting back to our rendezvous point and await the arrival of our transportation. I hope our driver will have the top up on the jeep. We'll have plenty of time if we hurry. I wouldn't want you to get your pretty dress all soaked in the rain. And this is the only dress uniform I have."

Mignonette glanced up at the tranquil blue sky overhead, from where the sun beat down brightly upon them. "You are incredible," she effused. And then mischievously teasing, "The moment of truth is near, my ambitious clairaudient!" She laughed and squeezed his hand. "I shall buy our dinner tonight, if you are right... and also publicly announce that I dedicate all of my love songs to you."

He too, laughed and squeezed her hand in return. "Now who's the one being ambitious? But if it's a wager we are making, both parties must risk a sacrifice. If my prediction is incorrect I will sing a duet with you, on stage and before the whole audience. That will be an event that Paris will long remember... along with the war. Which one will be considered as the least favorable, I dare not say!"

They were safely back at their cozy little cafe now, sitting inside receiving the velvet carpet treatment again and sipping wine while watching the sudden squall of rain that splashed against the windows as their jeep drove up with its canvas top raised in place.

CHAPTER TWO
A Grasp of Destiny

The next several days were busy ones for Major Kilmeade. He had several items of personal business to transact in addition to his military duties of preparation for the final decisive conflict, which was anticipated at any time now. He had always been a man of swift and sound decision, followed immediately by commensurate action. Carpe diem, seize the day, was his formula for success throughout his life. At the age of thirteen he had lost all known members of his family in the devastating earthquake of nineteen thirty- three, and had wisely invested the modest sum of money he inherited. By the time the war broke out he was an extremely wealthy and influential man. He was a lifetime member of the local yacht club and occupied a seat on the Governing Board of Officers.

With confirmed confidence in his judgment of the character of the woman he loved, and the pressing condition of circumstance, he wired an urgent message to his business agent in Los Angeles, to transfer a considerable sum of money immediately to the Paris bank, in the account of Mignonette Lescaut, with the stipulation that in event of his death, to transfer the remainder of his money and property into her name. He then apprised the Paris bank of the transaction, and opened an account for her.

Later on this day, with his mind now at much greater ease, he gave the evening charge of quarters the phone number where he could be reached in case of emergency, and had his driver take him to their nightclub a little early, to meet Mignonette, then dismissed him for the night.

Major Kilmeade sat alone at his table, as was his custom now since the beginning of his affaire d'amour with Mignonette, sipping his usual glass of vintage wine and listening to the melodious voice of his sweetheart singing her songs of love and inspiration.

At her first break she joined him, and after an affectionate greeting, they fell into serious discussion. He was the first to speak. He lowered his voice, "I have missed you so terribly all day, and I have something to say to you that I have wanted you to hear ever since we met! I believe you must surely know by now, as I have known from the first night I met you. I love you!" He rushed on, not waiting for a reply, so sure he was of her feelings for him. "I want to spend the rest of my life with you! Say what I want to hear, and we will be married tomorrow!" It was another moment of truth for them. Would he win again?

She was speechless from a great emotion, and could not give answer to the dearest question her heart had longed for. Taking charge of her momentary silence he added a further thought, more as an impulse, than to advantage his position, "You and I have had so little happiness, and perhaps so little time left to us now to enjoy it." (Was it possible his ears could also hear the future!) "If you love me as I love you, say what is in your heart... for I know it is there! Give me consent to make you mine!"

Her eyes were filled with tears of emotion as she struggled for speech and the magic word that would make her dream a reality! Momentarily overcome by a surge of unrepressed feelings, she responded with abandoned constraint, "Yes! Oh, yes, my darling! Take me! I am yours... and will always be! Je t'aime, mon cheri. Je t'aime!"

Disenchanted by the impairing aspect of their environs, and aware that their present unsecluded position was dysfunctional to the proper and much desired privacy demanded of that moment, and sensitive to the unwelcome attention their episodic romance had long invited, Kilmeade whispered a few words into the ear of his responsive companion, and they arose quickly, just as the orchestra struck up the strains of their favorite song: "Don't Sit Under The Apple Tree..." and with auspicious decorum, walked from the confining premises of the glittering cafe, out into the sheltering mantle of the Parisian night.

Without a word she led the way to a modest but scrupulously attended dwelling which she shared with an elderly couple. Without a word, close beside her, he followed! She placed a finger to her silent lips as they entered; and he nodded. Two minds, two hearts, with but one compelling desire of magnificent purpose! The world of man and his petty quarrels was shut away from them now. Theirs rested within the realm of God and His perfection, and was made of loving caresses and sweet moan! And God drew near and smiled as He beheld the scene dearest to His desire: the expression of loyal commitment to the awesome beauty of human love!

Time sped by, as is its wont when measured in increments of happiness, and they clung together now, close in each other's arms, and for a short period each lay in silent contemplation, enjoying the glory of their nearness and savoring the exquisite memory of requited paradise, and then at last shyly interchanging the sweet confidences of sacred intimacy.

Kilmeade was the first to speak. "I have always

believed the first time might be like this!" he whispered softly. "And oh, so well it has been worth the waiting!" Then added as he kissed her tenderly, "But reality exceeds my beautiful dream!"

The silence wasted between them as he anticipated her loving response. And then it came... and a great anger arose within him as he listened, mingling at once with an overwhelming feeling of sympathy and remorse! "It happened some years ago... right after the Huns took Paris!" She paused, dreading to go on. Would this make a difference in the way he felt for her, she wondered! She struggled on, knowing it had to be told now, if there was to be honor and truth between them. She was weeping softly as she continued, "It happened only that once. There was this officer, a brute of a man..." She paused again, shuddering at the painful memory.

Kilmeade interrupted her agony, "I've heard enough... too much! Just tell me his name! If he lives yet, he will die by the hand of the man whom you have chosen as your champion, and who has the rightful claim to your love! Tell me his name! I must kill him... and erase the stamp of shame he has put upon your honor! Do not deny me that!"

"I will never deny you anything... I love and honor you! But forgiveness is divine! Leave him to heaven!"

"A man cannot forgive that which is beyond forgiveness. If the insult had been to me, perhaps I could forgive, for it would then be mine to give. I live on this Earth, subject to the laws of my own conscience. Heaven can extract its pound of flesh after I have taken mine!" He was becoming impatient with her specious rationalization, almost gruffly demanding the man's identity again. "I must have his name! Any man who takes a woman by force, and defiles her chastity cannot be allowed to live and flout the honor God gave mankind! What say you!"

"I say, my love, your will be served. He was called by Major Hans Von Steubenfeld!" She smiled coquettishly, "My hero, you are so... so... gallant, so masculine, when you are angry... and I must confess I admire you for it!" They kissed... and the storm was over.

CHAPTER THREE
Fate

Some time later Kilmeade wakened suddenly from the throes of a disturbing dream, and arising in stealthy haste from the arms of his sleeping lover, called the charge of quarters to send his driver to pick him up at once. A troubling sound had invaded his dreams as he slept, a revelation... premonition, or clairaudience?

He dressed in hurried silence, and finding a writing pad on the night stand by the bed, he scribbled a brief note to Mignonette as he awaited his transportation. "My dearest one! Something has come up, urgent and unforeseen until now. Forgive me for leaving without awakening you, but you looked too happy to disturb. You would have wanted an explanation, and I had none I could give you. Keep the faith! We will have our life together! This is only au revoir! See you under the apple tree! Wait for me! I will come!"

He had barely finished, when he heard the jeep approaching. One last, adoring look he took of her face . . .as though it might be the last he would ever see, and then he stepped out into the barren night and closed the door quietly behind him, leaving her lying there alone, with her dreams of love, and the smile of God upon her lovely face.

Once outside, he rushed to the waiting jeep and leaped aboard. "Quick, Corporal!" he commanded in a subdued shout. "Take me to High Command Headquarters on the double – quick! Hell's about to break loose!"

"Yes sir," the startled man replied. The vehicle lunged forward with a roar and, racing at top speed, they were soon at their destination.

Kilmeade leaped from the still moving car and, taking the steps three at a time, rushed up and into the large building and abruptly accosted the sergeant on duty. "Quick, Sergeant! Get the General on the line! I must talk to him at once! Hurry!"

The sergeant stared at the major in consternation. "But... but he's asleep, sir," he stammered.

"Of course he is, you idiot! "Ring him! That's an order! Do it! Now!"

The man, somewhat crestfallen, quickly did as he was ordered. A voice came on the line, and Kilmeade snatched the phone from the startled noncom and delivered his urgent message in a voice that was respectful but convincing and forceful. "General, sir! This is Major Scott Kilmeade of the First Battalion, Second Division Headquarters. I have concrete information vital to the successful pursuance of this European campaign, and possibly to its victorious outcome. I must meet with you at once."

There was a split moment's silence, followed by some military profanity, then a short sentence, "I'm in room two zero four at the top of the stairs. Be here in one minute." There was a click on the line, followed by silence.

Kilmeade turned swiftly back to the man at the desk, "You did well, Sergeant. Carry on as you were."

He found the stairwell, and took the steps, three at a time again, and knocked on the designated door. "Come in, come in!" an impatient voice ordered.

Kilmeade seized the doorknob, but the door did not budge. "Sir, will you unlock your door, please. I have found entering a room is more easily accomplished that way."

Some more profanity, and then footsteps, and the door swung open. A tall man with graying hair, and half-dressed stood before him, scowling. The scowl left his face as he recognized Kilmeade. They had met in conversation several times before. The General was the officer who had recommended his Silver Stars. "Oh, it's you! Come on in, Major. I didn't place your name at first." His tone was apologetic. "What is this you are telling me?"

"Sir, the Germans are preparing to launch a peremptory attack in about an hour, as well as I can determine. Our troops on the front perimeters must be alerted at once or we will be subject to a disaster far worse than the Bulge. I cannot tell you in words you would believe, that this is absolutely true. You must trust me! That is why I have come to you. I knew you would be the one most likely to credit my unsubstantiated information, for you know me as a man of honor. And I repeat to you now: what I am telling you is the absolute truth. I shall put on record what I have told you, and the solution I recommend!" He paused and looked hard at the man he knew he must convince. "If I am wrong, surely you must know I will stand for general court-martial. And if there is a possibility I am right, it is unconscionable that you do not act upon this information. The consequences are too dire to consider any alternative." He paused for rhetorical effect, poising for the coup de grace, then swept on to the conclusion. "One has but to compute the waste in dedicated human lives and precious time because we did not address the probability of counterattack before the battle of the Bulge. If you will recall, sir, I said then, that it would happen... just as it did. But no one would listen. Will anyone listen now? I tell you it will happen again." As he spoke these last words he knew he had won.

The incredulous expression on the General's face had vanished. "It shall be done as you say, Major. You have convinced me I have been listening to a man with an exceptional mind and judgment, and an impeccable sense of honor."

Kilmeade was filled with overpowering relief. "You have my greatest gratitude and admiration, sir." Then smiled as he added in a somewhat lighter tone, "If you knew the whole truth of the sacrifice I have made to tell you all this, you would surely recommend me for the Medal of Honor." His reference was to Mignonette and the precious hours with her he had forsaken. Indeed, if he had known the whole truth of what it was to cost both of them he would surely have wept.

When Kilmeade left Division Headquarters he raced back to his regiment and found that word of the impending German counterattack had already been received, and adequate measures were being swiftly implemented along the entire perimeter of the allied front. There would be no repetition of the debacle of the Bulge. This time they would be ready. "God bless the General," he thought, "and thank God for all good men! I'll tell him the source of my information after this is all over," he chuckled. "His profanity is an accomplishment to be envied, and an experience to marvel upon! Even 'Old Blood and Guts' takes a back seat to him in that regard."

He stood now alongside the regimental commander, Colonel Wyatt, studying the elaborate layout table of tactical maps, and scanning the strategic positions occupied by their regimental personnel. Suddenly a startled expression came into his face! "Colonel, sir, quickly... we must concentrate our strength here," pointing to a spot on the map. "Before it is too late. They will be coming through this gap. They are concentrating here... with tanks and heavy artillery!" Pointing again, "We must move these troops over, from here," pointing, "to this position! We haven't much time! Maybe twenty minutes at the outside!"

The Colonel gave him a startled look. "We can't do that, Major. It will make us vulnerable at the point of removal."

"Trust what I say, sir. They will not attack at that point! It is here," pointing again... "I know. You must trust me. It is what the divisional general has ordered. Call him... he will verify what I have told you." He strode from the room. He knew the man had a streak of stubbornness, and there was no time to argue. At the motor pool he commandeered a loaded weapons carrier, settled in the driver's seat and set off at top speed for the front lines.

Fifteen minutes flashed by, that seemed like hours to the beleaguered officer, and the miles lay in smoke behind him. At last he reached his destination and discovered, to his intense relief, that several companies of infantry were in the process of repositioning on the double to the point where Kilmeade had designated on the map the Germans would concentrate their attack. The General's confirmation had supported him once more!

He picked up enough men to comprise six two-man bazooka teams, and armed them from the weapons he carried in his vehicle, then sped on for the short distance remaining. Optimally, to repulse the initial tank attack he expected, he would have preferred the armored support that was on the way, but he knew it would not arrive in time. Until then, they must do the best with what they had available.

The day remained as quiet as death! But the advent of that specter loomed imminent, and would strike with lightning swiftness and the sound of thunder. Countless valiant men would die! At such a time it is a blessing to be brave, for the taste of death is savored only once by men of valor... and these men had made peace with their God on the historic beaches of bloody Normandy! They would die with honor and distinction . . .every man a hero!

In muffled swiftness Kilmeade placed his bazooka teams in strategic positions, his focus of attention simultaneously directed beyond the immediate front, into the depth of the German ranks, listening for any pertinent sound that would advantage his cause. He detected a large concentration of men and equipment poised, he knew, for immediate attack. He had the word passed all along the line, "Be ready. They will be coming at any moment."

He suddenly glanced expectantly upward and behind him. "Our bombers are only moments away. Pass the word! That should minimize the effect of their heavy artillery." His heart was filled with optimistic hope again, for the success of the allied campaign, and the safety of his buddies in arms.

And then, as swiftly as his hope had arisen, it sank again. Somewhere in the distant direction of the enemy's massed forces a chilling sound came to him . . .the unmistakable grating swish of an artillery shell slipping into the breach of a huge artillery gun! And the slamming of the breech. And then another, and another! He leaped up from cover, and in desperation ran along behind the entrenched positions of his men, shouting, "Take cover! Keep down! Enemy artillery fire is coming. A barrage! Enemy armor will be sure to follow close!" Like a great warrior out of the pages of history he towered above the scene of battle, resolute and without fear, his only concern: the success of his mission and the safety of his beloved men! Shades of Horatius at the Tiber bridge! "Dear God," he prayed, "Not Normandy again."

And then the pandemonium of Kilmeade's world stood still, rendered motionless in space and time... a tabloid frozen with punishing clarity in the recesses of his mind! Years later the reality of those last moments would return to him in memory: The sky, dark with planes silhouetted in thunder overhead; the sight of huge enemy tanks, living machines of death, hurtling in snarling assault upon their entrenched positions from the bluff above: the high-pitched whine of their own tanks coming up from their rear! And then the devastating explosion of a huge artillery shell somewhere near him! That was all... and then oblivion!

No, that was not quite all! At the instant the shell fragment struck him, another thought had forged its way into his mind and engraved itself there indelibly... his last: With the shock of great remorse and guilt he became aware he had placed in jeopardy the happiness of the girl who loved him, notwithstanding his own. "Mignonette, forgive me. Mignonette!" And that, by the Grace of God, was the catalyst that would one day return his life to him. That, and the Apple Tree!

CHAPTER FOUR
Interlude

And then they came... the enemy! In a little less than two hours, just as Kilmeade had predicted, the Germans launched their attack. It was the fiercest of the war in the few hours that it sustained. And the Allies would surely have been driven back from their favorable position with great loss of personnel, and perhaps have had to vacate Paris if they had not been forewarned and thus ably prepared.

On the edge of that fateful dawn, the echoing thunder of heavy artillery again rocked the great city of Paris. Every citizen was shaken from peaceful slumber by the threatening recurrence of impending doom. And they trembled in fear of the outcome.

Back at the love cottage, the happy delights of Mignonette's maidenly dreams reluctantly faded from her assailed slumbers, her subconscious mind yielding to the inimical dissonance of minatory sound. Instinctively she groped in the darkness for the comfort of her lover's proximity, only to find, to her disquieting surprise, he was no longer beside her.

She switched on the bedside lamp and glanced hopefully around the small room. Her heart sank as she noted his clothes were gone from the chair where she had folded and placed them. And then her glance fell on the note lying on the night stand. Seizing it, she tremulously read and reread the fateful, scrawled contents. And as she pondered the message, her mind probed for the truth behind the succinct words, and her heart was filled with a great dread for the dire possibility it implied. She believed he could not have received information from any military source, for she would have heard the phone ring. No, some way it had to be that inscrutable clairaudience of his again! But she would not abandon hope yet, for she felt sure he would not sacrifice their new-found happiness in pursuit of a frivolous exploit. And then the distant thunder of heavy artillery smote in upon her awareness again, its ponderous echoes vibrating the building and accentuating the clear and irrefutable truth she was denying: The sound of cannon explained his absence! Caught up in the anticipation of disaster and the throes of stark despair, she broke down in violent weeping!

CHAPTER FIVE
The Ordeal

Scott Kilmeade sat there with his friend, physician and personal attendant at the table on the sidewalk cafe with his brooding thoughts, his mind striving to reclaim his elusive memory and resurrect his broken life. As the afternoon wore on, pale shadows crept silently from the buildings along the busy walkway bordering the strand, shadows he could not see, but rather sensed from the growing coolness of the air.

Irresponsive to his efforts, the baffling incontinuity of episodic time continued to dangle before him like the terminus of a broken link, its frayed end hanging in the vacuity of space. Did this signify he had come to the end of his rope! His concentration for the last several hours was relegated to sounds confined within the limits of his crippled memory... among them, the music of a dear voice that assailed his heart with tears . . .one beautiful and deathless song whose words and tune he could not quite capture, something about an apple tree. He did not know why it affected him so poignantly. He could only suppose it must have some direct connection with the girl, Mignonette, whose image had flashed into his mind back in America, giving him the initial intimation of who he had been and who he now was!

His mind then began to wander in the sparse and strangely nostalgic pastures of his dormant memory. He gave it free and welcome rein. It was his way of bringing back, a little at a time, selective incidents from his stubbornly evasive past. The damaged tissues of his brain were responding more favorably each day to the practice of this exercise. More distant memories returned to him first. He could clearly remember many incidents that had occurred during his childhood and in his high school days.

However, as a result of his severe injury he had temporarily lost the awareness of his spiritual gift, the ability that had enabled him to detect and interpret phenomena beyond the natural scope of sentient achievement, and which now remained latent but recoverable within his consciousness. And although the last ten years of his life were still a complete mystery to him, he knew there had been a girl... he had seen her in his. And he knew they had loved because his heart had told him so. For, in every honest heart where love has dwelt, there abides a truth that cannot be forsworn, no matter the disposition of the mind!

The while, Dr. Richards, for the most part, had sat silently by, allowing his charge, under his watchful eye, to enjoy the uninterrupted freedom of his own thoughts. It was the natural mending process adopted and increasingly practiced by specialists of that era; and results were predominately encouraging. What surprised the doctor was that his patient had discovered this procedure by himself, a fact that, by itself alone, would suggest at least the hopeful possibility of a partial recovery, if not a complete one.

Richards spoke softly then, hesitant to interrupt any vital train of his patient's therapeutic thought process, "Colonel, you have an appointment tomorrow afternoon in Paris, and it's getting late. It's been a long afternoon, and you need your rest. The series of tests they put you through will be particularly trying. Believe me, I know. And if you are well rested, your reactions and responses will be more voluntary, conducive to a more accurate and comprehensive diagnosis."

Kilmeade smiled, something he rarely did anymore. "I never argue with doctors and salesmen," he replied. "And you impress me as the paragon of both. Let's shove off, Mate!"

Back aboard his yacht, Kilmeade went immediately to bed and, able to control his conscious mind, soon fell into a deep and restful sleep.

The next few days were spent undergoing involved tests given by a team of brain specialists, after which their prognosis was optimistic for eventual recovery. They saw no necessity for surgery. However, they did strongly recommend he remain in the proximate vicinity where he had spent his last days prior to his injury. They felt that some seemingly insignificant but familiar phenomenon might advantage the recovery of his memory, and could do no harm. Otherwise it might take an indeterminate number of years before his complete memory regained its normal function. His blindness was another matter. They believed that only after extensive exploratory surgery would they be able to offer any kind of constructive opinion, and even then, very likely none at all. Their final suggestion left the door to hope yet slightly ajar: There was a surgeon in Switzerland, they said, a former army officer, who had performed miracles in restoring sight to a few wounded war veterans. Perhaps he might help. It was certainly worth investigating. Dr. Richards took it under consideration.

Needless to say, this therapeutic advice regarding his memory was quickly agreed to by both men, and immediately adopted, as Kilmeade had become desperately assailed by the nagging persistence of a sound within his mind that seemed to be telling him a dear and troubled heart needed him, pressing, imploring him to remember the significance of the illusory melody that haunted him constantly now... a song about an apple tree! He must talk about this to Dr. Richards. He wondered now, why he had not thought of that before. But he never had. His friend might be able to tell him something that would help. He had been an army doctor during the war. Yes, he would certainly know something about the war that might prove familiar to Kilmeade and assist in orienting his memory. And so these two veterans began an ongoing therapeutic dialogue, the topic being primarily based on Kilmeade's personal military record, which Richards had studiously consulted, and that of his army unit, encompassing the initial invasion at Omaha Beach to the final engagement at Meaux, just beyond Paris, where he had suffered the wound that obliterated his memory, his sight, and his life! And included, stronger than all these, his love that had endured!

Sunning themselves now, pool-side at the private inn where they had taken lodging, they talked. And piece by piece increments of Kilmeade's life slowly flowed back into his consciousness as he listened to the incredible and revealing tale his attendant imparted! "Your records show you were a second lieutenant at the landing, but the shortage of officers because of extensive casualties, and your demonstration of outstanding leadership hastened your final promotion to major some time before the occasion of your wound during the decisive battle at Meaux. Your records indicate that through the great confusion involved at that time you were listed as `Missing in Action'. You were brought to the field hospital minus `dog tags,' so you were registered as `identity unknown.' When you were shipped to the States it was there that I fortunately recognized and identified you. Your fingerprints were subsequently taken, and my testimony was thereby substantiated." Richards paused, but his listener knew the man's story was not yet finished.

"Tell me," Kilmeade said. "How were you able to recognize me? Where had you seen me before?"

"I had a picture of you, a photograph my younger brother had sent me. You were in a group together, taken in England just before D-Day. One of those Silver Stars you have pinned to your tunic was awarded you for 'heroism, above and beyond.' You saved my brother's life on the beach at Normandy, a Corporal Richards!" He paused again, a paroxysm of emotion making speech difficult. After a moment he continued, "I thought I would never be able to express my overwhelming gratitude to you. But fate sometimes plays strange tricks. And when I saw you at the hospital in New York, I vowed I would repay you, whatever it took. And so I will! That is why I am sitting here with you now. Together you and I will somehow restore your memory and eyesight if it is possible! Until then, I will always be at your side. My brother is my only living relative. If I had lost him, I would have had nothing to live for. By your heroism, at the risk of your own life, you secured my life for me! I can do no less than make every effort to give yours back to you! To do otherwise would be a monstrous sin... against the God who endowed you with the indomitable courage to answer His call, and against the man who acted as His instrument of mercy! I am blessed to know and serve you, Colonel Kilmeade."

There were tears in the eyes of the man who spoke perceptively but was unseen. And there were tears in the eyes behind the dark glasses of the man who listened with undiminished perception but could not see. For such as this, is the compassion of noble men. And such as this, is the nobility of men of compassion. Honor bestows vitality to life, and enhances the growth of the soul.

Kilmeade sat silent for a moment, fighting back the wave of emotion that his friend's words had stirred within him. Dedicated loyalty of such immense proportions almost embarrassed him, and he was suddenly caught in a vortex of ethereal transcendency that left him momentarily speechless! Gathering his thoughts at last, and returning the conversation to a more rational theme, he managed, "You addressed me as colonel, just now... and yesterday. Yet you have said I was a major at the time I was wounded. Is there any special significance in that... anything that might help restore my memory, that I should be told?"

"I don't think so. That all happened after you were wounded. But I'll tell you the circumstances. It's regarding a great honor awarded you, and you have a right to know. Some military officer of highest rank... reputedly General Eisenhower, himself, ordered you be given the Congressional Medal of Honor... so your record indicates, and promoted to full colonel! It had something to do with a miracle – a mysterious, yet reliable allusion to information you gave that turned the tide of the Allied war effort and assured an outstanding victory at the final great battle near Meaux. No one seems to know what really happened. The answer to that secret lies sequestered within the archives of your flawed memory."

He paused a moment, trying to recall all he had learned from his meticulous study of Kilmeade's war record. "You were also awarded the Croix de Guerre and the Legion of Honor by the French government for the same action!" His voice was redolent with a profusion of pride and awe for the man whose deeds of outstanding valor and sacrifice had meant so much for so many!

As Kilmeade listened, his beleaguered mind began a fierce struggle with the tortuous past... reaching desperately into the darkness of his broken life... grasping in wild random, to capture the shadows that swept like elusive phantoms across the vacant platen of his brain, his face contorted into the semblance of a grotesque mask of pain! He writhed in futile agony, his powerful hands clutching at the empty air. "So near!" he cried. "So near, and so hopeless. Dear God, help me. My beautiful Mignonette, she weeps for me. She believes I am dead and lost to her. How cruel... how needlessly, desperately cruel." He fell to sobbing.

Richards, caught up in the young man's paroxysm of grief, unbearable even to him, put an arm around his shoulder. "Come," he said, gently, "You must rest now. It is enough for this day. We will try again tomorrow. I think we have made some progress. We will find your Mignonette! You must be patient." He led his charge to their rooms, and assisted him to bed, where Kilmeade soon fell into a strange and troubled slumber.

For five long and vacant years, his natural, intrinsic power of subconscious sensory perception had been deprived of its luxury to dream. But now, the cruelty of inexorable reality, thrust into his consciousness earlier that day as a therapeutic process, had stimulated and activated his mind, reaching into and reviving tissues of his injured brain. Up from his disentombed mind and into his dithyrambic dreaming, like a great storm, the ancient past swept in upon him with devastating force.

First came the thunder of heavy artillery fire; then the rumble and mingling whine of heavy tanks from the bluff above him and from the rear of this place where his dream had now taken him! Overhead the sky was dark with aircraft! Everywhere the atmosphere was overwhelmed with a poisonous, minatory sound and a great darkness spread over the world around him, like black rain... and he was falling... falling, catapulted into the nothingness of eternal oblivion, alive in death. And that was all!

No, that was not nearly all. That was just the beginning! There was the plaguing memory of a beautiful woman, and the searing anguish of a great regret for a risk he had taken, that if lost, would destroy her happiness... a risk it was his duty to take, for only he could do it... And it had to be done! "Forgive me, my precious Mignonette!"

A great light arose in the east... brighter than a thousand suns! And Scott Kilmeade knew that is the way it had been at the first sunrise on the first day God had created the world! And there was a tree... an apple tree... standing in the center of a garden. It was the Tree of Life... And this was the Garden of Delight was Eden. And a beautiful maiden was sitting there alone beneath its sheltering boughs, with an expression of sadness and hope upon her lovely face... Waiting for a dream. Could it be Eve? No, it was his own Mignonette!

A catharsis of momentous proportions was transpiring within the long-wasted and febrile mind of Scott Kilmeade, the cathexis principal... instinctively activated in obedience to his enduring trust in a precious icon... his unshakable belief in the fidelity of the sacred oath they had exchanged, and the beloved apple tree.

As he lay there now, a great peace suffused his soul. He had come back into his life... all the way back. The vision had been a message from God that He had answered his prayer. The brilliant and beloved tableau faded slowly from his sight; but he knew that one day soon, the vision would be replicated in reality, and he would be standing there under the apple tree, with love in his arms. He sank into a deep and restful sleep at last... the first in five years. There was a smile on the face of God! There was a smile in the heart of a grateful hero. And hopefully there would soon be a smile to replace the ravaging shadow lowering over the steadfast heart of a despairing lover!

CHAPTER SIX
The Magnificent Quest

All day the thunder of war shook the tenor and threatened the peace again, of a beleaguered city! All day the sky over Paris was darkened with aircraft, the streets teeming with vehicles of war! And all day the citizens cowered indoors in numb silence, awed by the renewed threat of an unspeakable disaster they had supposed would never come again!

And Mignonette... what of her? Could she be brave again, with so much more to lose now? Her fear was no longer for herself, but for the dear one in danger, who was all of life to her! For that is the way of a maiden in love! She knew in her heart that he would be in the vanguard of the terrible battle that was raging around them, for he was a warrior... and a champion!

For two days these ancient enemies were locked in a struggle for supremacy at the brink of a trembling Paris, and then the awesome might and savage determination of the Allies prevailed, and the redoubtable foe was contained and thrown back. The Americans continued their irresistible onslaught, and in a month the war in Europe against the evil Axis war machine was over! And the format for a greater and more deadly threat to the sovereignty of a noble and democratic world society was created: The cold war with Russia and her evil communist philosophy. But that's another story, for another time.

Those first few days of the initial engagement fought in the vicinity of Meaux, took their toll on the emotions of a distraught Mignonette. Each day she would visit the hastily constructed and over-crowded hospitals around the Paris area where the wounded personnel were first taken, searching for her beloved, helping when needed and tirelessly seeking any information she could acquire regarding his status. At the end of each day she would seek refuge in her small room, relieved that she had not found him among the many casualties, but increasingly disturbed that she had discovered no trace of him.

At the outset of the intended surprise counterattack by the Axis there had been only a momentary threat of breakthrough in the forward lines of the Allied front as a result of Kilmeade's timely information, and the Axis invasion attempt had been quickly blunted and hurled back in confusion. Some semblance of order was soon established and the list of purported casualties was posted as public information at each hospital.

Each day Mignonette would read the list of names of the known dead, with eyes that searched for the dreaded truth she hoped not to find! His name was never there! With renewed hope she would read on. Nor was his name ever among the wounded! She would breath a great sigh of relief, and turn away. He was not dead! He had not been wounded. He was still all right... and safe.

And then one day her eyes caught the bottom of the page, where a few additional names were posted. MIA, the caption read. And then at last she saw his name... the name of her beloved! MIA... What did that mean? Her heart began racing, dreading the answer!

"It means `missing in action'," a nurse nearby told her.

"Is that bad?" she wondered.

"Not necessarily," the nurse answered. "It simply means there has been a SNAFU in the records, somewhere along the line. They have just lost official track of him for the moment." She gave Mignonette an inquiring look. "Say, Missy, aren't you that young lady that sings in the evenings at the nightclub on the Rue de laPaix?"

"Yes," Mignonette replied, "but they have closed for a while. It's the war, again. It is so close!"

"And this young man you are looking for... is he that handsome major you have been romancing, and that Paris is gossiping about?"

"Yes." And then, "I suppose," she added. "I mean, there has been a little talk..."

"Yes, indeed!" the nurse smiled. And then added, solemnly, "I wish you and your young man good luck... and happiness!" She continued with her chores.

That night, in the refuge of her little room, as she sat alone with her thoughts, reviewing the harrowing episode at the hospital and contemplating the baffling complexity of her state of affairs, a feeling of great weariness and frustration suddenly seized her. How hopeless everything now seemed! How different it was now, from that night which though hardly a week ago, now seemed like forever.

Her eyes wandered absently about the room, reconstructing in her mind that immortal scene again, as she had done so often before: Over in the far corner, across from her, stood the neatly made-up single bed that had served as an accommodation for their commitment of sacred love to one another. And beside it was the chair where she had placed his neatly folded clothes. How fresh and clean he had smelled. How masculine he was! How strong, yet gentle and tender.

As she thus idly reminisced, an object suddenly caught her eye she had not noticed before, something small and shiny hanging, half hidden, from the back of the same chair. Her curiosity aroused, she retrieved it and immediately realized it was Kilmeade's metal identification tags he had worn around his neck on a chain. In his preoccupied haste to leave, that last fateful evening they had spent together, he had overlooked them. "I'll give them to him the next time we meet," she told herself. How vital they would have been to him at that moment, she would one day learn! How long it would be until they met again, if ever, she was fortunate, at that time, not to know. In every life worth living there is a rainbow. Remove hope, and there is nothing.

The sound of the terrible guns she blamed for her loss, were further away each day, echoing mockingly in the growing distance, punishing her belief of their ultimate happiness together. They had loved too deeply for it to ever die! Her lover had been too strong and vital, too beautiful and brave to succumb to ordinary death! And so she clung to her hope with desperate fervor and unabiding and unshakable faith. Her evenings, she spent singing at the Golden Peacock Cafe on the Rue de la Paix. But no word of the fate of her lover ever came to her!

She ended her performance each evening with her signature song as her final number: 'Don't Sit Under The Apple Tree With Anyone Else But Me.' The packed audience always gave her a standing ovation, for all of Paris knew her pathetic story by now: how she spent her time each day tirelessly searching for news of her lover, wherever it might lead her, and coming quietly home each evening, no closer to the happiness she had lost! For that reason, as much as for the beauty of her voice and appearance, the Golden Peacock Cafe had become the most popular nightclub in the City of

Lights.

And then one fine day she simultaneously received news of two separate and monumental events that served to ameliorate the haunting sadness of her existence and optimistically alter her perspective regarding the future: She was notified by the Bank of Paris that a large amount of money had been deposited by Kilmeade into an account for her; and the same day, her doctor had verified her suspicion that she was with child! She wept with happiness, for it sustained her steadfast belief that the father of her child, her lover, would come to her, should it ever become possible. She was remembering those vows of undying love they had exchanged, and those impassioned words of tenderness they had spoken: "If you do not come, I will be there still... waiting. There will be no other love for me." And his reply, "If I live, and am able, I will surely come." Each night upon going to bed, she would recite to herself that deathless dialogue as a mantra to dispel the haunting, careworn thoughts of the day, and to beguile elusive slumber. Fate may have dealt her a difficult hand, but God would guide her in its play.

And so, preparing for the day when maternal responsibilities would dominate the major part of her time and attention, indeed, her life, she bought a small cottage on several acres of land near the city of Lausanne in Switzerland, taking up residence there and becoming a Swiss citizen. She had no wish to risk the anguish of another war, for though it had been the fortunes of a war that had brought love into her life, it had also taken it away. She would live out the remainder of her life in a neutral country free from the threat of any cataclysmic disruption.

Mignonette was a wealthy woman now. The sum of

money that Kilmeade had deposited in her account was upward of one million dollars, United States currency. She immediately employed an experienced older woman as a live-in maid and housekeeper, with nursing experience for the approaching blessed event, when her services would be of vital necessity. A little later, after she had drawn up the basic plans for its design, she contacted an eminent architectural landscape gardener and had him initiate the construction, or rather, the idyllic creation, of the garden that was to replicate into reality and immortalize, the beauty and the truth of her beloved apple tree. This would facilitate and thus hasten her lover's return... she was sure. "I must believe with all my heart that this is true," she would tell herself, "and it will happen! It must not be otherwise."

And she would visualize that when he came, he would find her sitting there beneath their tree, waiting... just as she had sworn so passionately, so long ago. A tiny, blue-eyed child would be playing at her feet. And he would look up and say to her in his lisping baby prattle, "Mamma, is that Daddy? Has he come?" How comforting it was to her, to imagine such an optimal scene of happiness! It was the best of what she had, to sustain her hope through the traumatic ordeal of her loneliness!

The halcyon days of spring came in Mignonette's valley. All the trees were in full blossom, and the grassy hills were green with new life. The terrible war was over now, and a fragile peace lay ungently upon the restless world once more. Her garden was completed at last, and the piece de resistance that stood in its center was heavy with fruit. And she was heavy with child. Then autumn came, and the time for harvest was near.

It was a warm morning in early autumn as

Mignonette, sitting sidesaddle atop her favorite gentle-gaited mare, took her morning constitutional, accompanied as usual by the woman who acted as her companion, maid servant and nurse. Their horses had just crested a hill a mile or two from her property, when a flock of wild fowl, startled by the unexpected appearance of horse and rider, sprang into the air in noisy flight, panicking Mignonette's mount who was in the lead. With a terrified snort, the horse bolted recklessly down the far side of the rise, with Mignonette desperately trying to maintain her seat atop the animal, while also attempting to check its hazardous pace. Her companion, riding in the more secure astride manner, instinctively spurred after her in futile pursuit, to assist in preventing her possible injury. Her attention was focused on following a slower but more judicious downhill zigzag course to avoid the hazardous plight of her mistress, and so she could only watch helplessly and in horror as Mignonette's horse, in attempting to abruptly halt its flight at the bottom of the steep incline, stumbled and fell, unseating its fragile rider, and throwing her heavily to the ground, clear of the animal's thrashing hooves.

The maid reined her mount to a sliding stop and leaping from the saddle, she ran to where her mistress lay unconscious. "Oh, Missy!" she cried in a sobbing voice. "Oh, my poor, dear Missy. What has happened to you?"

Receiving no answer, she ran to a stream nearby, and wetting her handkerchief, returned and applied it to the girl's forehead. Mignonette still gave no sign of response.

At a loss as to what to do, she glanced further on across the grassy landscape for help. About a half mile away she descried a large dwelling enclosed in an elaborate courtyard. Mounting her horse hastily, she set out for it at a gallop.

She rang the doorbell frantically and a maid opened the door immediately. "Please, can you help me? My mistress has been thrown by her horse and is badly injured. Down there... by the stream!"

The woman reacted as though she were conversant with such emergencies, "Wait here. I will get the doctor." She disappeared, and a tall, professional looking young man soon appeared.

"May I be of assistance, madam?" he asked. "Exactly what is your situation?" His manner was direct but his tone of voice was gentle and concerned.

"We, my mistress and I, were out riding, when suddenly her horse was frightened by a flock of birds, and bolted. Her horse fell and she was unseated and fell hard! She is unconscious and I couldn't revive her. You will need a carriage to transport her. Oh, please, can you hurry. I had to leave her unattended! I must get back to her!" She paused, and as a necessary afterthought added, "She is seven months pregnant! Oh, I am so worried!"

"Go back to her at once," the man ordered. "I will be along immediately!" He disappeared inside, and Mignonette's maid sprang astride her horse and returned in haste to wait at her mistress' side, who still lay unconscious where she had fallen.

In a few short minutes an ambulance sped from the hospital to where the maid anxiously waited, and the doctor and his nurse emerged and hurried to where Mignonette lay. After a quick check of her pulse and breathing, and then assisted by both women, he placed her carefully on a stretcher and put her into the ambulance. "It is likely I will have to operate," he said, as he got into his vehicle. "And I might need your assistance. You can stable your horses at my place for the time being. Bring them along. My man will take charge of them when you arrive, and my nurse will prepare you for the operating room. I'll see you in a few minutes. We must hurry. There's no time to lose." And so, with his nurse carefully sitting in attendance of his new patient, he drove back to the hospital.

The doctor was in the operating room now, where his nurse and Mignonette's maid, who was also an accredited nurse, had prepared Mignonette for intensive examination. In the recent aftermath of the war many women had become competent and skilled nurses, and these two were excellent proof of this.

A scant half hour had elapsed since Mignonette's accident and the conclusion of the doctor's diagnosis. "I must take her child by Cesarean section immediately if either is to have a chance of survival," he finally announced. "The mother is hemorrhaging profusely internally, and the baby will soon drown! Let's get to work!"

The operation was touch and go for some long and anxious moments, but by the end of an hour mother and child were safely out of danger and sleeping peacefully in the recovery room. It was obvious that the doctor was an unusually gifted surgeon. "What a beautiful boy," he had remarked of his tiny patient. "The father must have been a handsome fellow! And the mother is certainly a beautiful woman."

The doctor and his nurses, after cleaning up, were lounging in the doctor's office relaxing from their intense and dedicated labor while sipping wine and getting acquainted. "You're an American, aren't you?" the doctor had just asked of Mignonette's nurse.

"Yes," she replied. "I was an army nurse during the war. My name is Susan Johnson. Susie, to my friends," she added, smiling.

"Susie, it is then," he replied.

The doctor's nurse smiled and nodded agreement; then replied, "I am called Maria Shumacher... just plain Maria, to my friends." She laughed at her obvious appropriation of Nurse Susan's amiable gesture of camaraderie. She continued her introductory remarks, her voice taking on a more serious tone. "I too, was an army nurse... a different army, perhaps, but I served where I was needed! We are all, more or less, pawns to compulsive circumstance, and I make no apology for the role fate cast for me. My only choice was to serve the needs of humanity. And, as now, that is what I did." She sighed, and the others understood. "Those of us whose lives have not been sacrificed on the alter of power, must endure to amend the wrongs so long afflicted upon the innocents of this world!" She paused, smiling wryly. "Forgive me, but I also cannot help thinking of those of us who yet remain and continue to feel the great sorrow for the ones we have loved and lost. And we must also remember and give obeisance to the heroes who have survived!" There was a hint of moisture in her eyes as she concluded her speech... which only served to substantiate that everyone had lost someone!

There was a temporary lull in the conversation, as all were momentarily lost in their own personal thoughts. At last the doctor spoke, "It seems that a revelation of my mysterious past is now in order. Suffice it to say my name is Hans Vandermeer. Some of my friends of the past," he smiled, "have referred to me as Doctor Wunderbar, I am flattered to say." He hesitated, as though carefully preparing his choice of words, and then continued. "I too, serve where I am most needed. And I too, seek to amend the malfeasance of evil and the damage of misfortune, by the use of medicine and surgery." He paused again, and then succinctly concluded, "My skills cover all phases of surgery, but my specialty is the brain.

"I have but recently relocated here and implemented my own medical facility, in order to more freely execute my individual, enlightened methods, and thus better serve the needy and infirm... which will explain why we here are as yet understaffed."

The personal introductions and explanations having been taken care of now, they addressed their attention to the present, and consideration of the patients. For the next few days one of the three would be required to be attendant at the bedside of their charges at all times. "And we must always wear a sterile gown and gloves when attending them," the doctor reminded, "and a mask... to avoid contamination. The woman is especially vulnerable at this period of time, for her immune system has been particularly reduced. And also, the child is premature, and will be confronted with weakened resistance."

For some inexplicable reason, the doctor did not question into the history of his adult patient. Perhaps the patent phenomena that met his tutored eye was sufficient for adequate diagnosis. It is beyond question that the man saw things others could not see! Or perhaps had experienced things that others could not know!

Each passing day the two skilled nurses

administered to the needs of their recuperating patients. And each day, the doctor changed her dressings. And always they wore their masks and freshly laundered surgical gowns ... as prescribed. The child, robust in spite of his immaturity, thrived on the special formula concocted by the doctor, for Mignonette was not lactating, due to the unseasonal early birth, and was unable to nurse him.

As for Mignonette, her condition had favorably progressed to the degree that she was discharged from the hospital at the end of two weeks, and permitted to return home. At the beginning of the second week she was entirely under the care of the two nurses, and they had abandoned use of their surgical masks, although they were always attired in meticulously laundered sanitary gowns. She saw no more of her brilliantly gifted redeeming angel, the wunderbar surgeon! She was told that he was deeply preoccupied in acquiring a selective group of doctors and nurses to advance his ambitious plans to staff what he hoped would become the premier surgical hospital in Switzerland... or indeed, the world. Was the man obsessed? Or was he on a great crusade? Or was it both... a colossal dedication aimed at contrition for the soul. This great world is a small place when giants walk the land!

Mignonette was back home now, sitting in rapture under her apple tree each day, weather permitting, cradling in her ecstatic arms a vibrant and cooing mite of love! And the nursery song she crooned to rest his infant slumbers was an old and deathless melody, once a musical tribute sung by the noble warriors who fought and died for a great cause, and offered now in faith to the loves they left behind, as a lullaby to the product of that love: "Don't Sit Under The Apple Tree With

Anyone Else But Me." Her happiness was halfway complete. The noble mantra of their vows, so oft repeated, was effecting its cause. God was in His heaven. All was well with her world.

CHAPTER SEVEN
The Sound of Drums

Two dark and dominating thoughts assailed the newly reclaimed latent and proliferating memory of Scott Kilmeade as he lay on a lounge by their hotel pool sunning himself... two excruciating imputations that infused his mind alternately with the extravagant passions of hate and love. Two separate moral transgressions that demanded a justice peremptorily circumscribed by one single stroke of a capricious and vacillating fate.

The first was induced by his unrequited gratification of vengeance for the inflicted stain of an unconscionable sin. The other, more benign in aspect, yet of primary and more desperate importance, begged redress to the woman who had committed her love to him implicitly, and who had then been cruelly and summarily bereft of her happiness... As had he of his.

Which of the two he would reasonably attend first, rested entirely to the discretion of that same whimsical fate... For he had no clue, as yet, to the whereabouts of either, so busily was he occupied in recollecting and assembling the fragments of his shattered existence. However, his compelling desire to reestablish his loving relationship with Mignonette, to assuage her agony of deprivation and loneliness, and to reaffirm his oath of undying loyalty to their love, importuned him to direct his initial efforts in that direction.

The other matter could reasonably await the prognosis of his optical injury, and the remote possibility of his regaining his sight. Although he knew, in the final analysis, even his continued blindness would not be a factor in deterring his original decision to extract vengeance for the heinous violation of Mignonette's maidenhood, and subsequently reduce the virulence of its stigma to a somewhat less intolerable degree. It was to him, an open wound, which he knew, if left untreated would never heal.

Kilmeade's uncanny sense of hearing was fast returning, and as he lay there now with his mind desperately probing the familiar aspects of the past, struggling to breech the clouded barrier of those lost years for a useful clue, he would instinctively pause momentarily to interrupt his thought, and direct his attention to the immediate sounds around him... and to one sound in particular: an icon that had given his life back to him... a song they both had loved, from the war years: The sweet, nostalgic song about an apple tree. If she lived yet, and if she still loved as once she had, he knew she would be singing, as she had promised... and he would hear/ And he would come!

He felt the suffusing rays of the summer sun as it spread its warmth over him, but no light penetrated into the stygian darkness of his barren sight! In the fervor of his mounting anguish he cried out, "Oh, call to me, my precious Mignonette, that my heart may once more feel the brilliance of your love. The Earth can have its sterile sun, that shines no more for me. To claim a needed respite from the ravages of night, it is you, and only you that I must have. Sing for me, the song I love, and I will seek and find you, wherever you may be. I can abide my world of darkness, but I will not live without your love." His eyes had lost the power to see, but not the will to weep. But tears cannot wash away the pain within one's heart, no matter the volume of their flow.

As he lay there in the anguish of his grief, struggling for a rationale of emotional tranquility, suddenly, out of the torpid summer air a transient breeze, as though in response to his fervent plea, touched his face and cooled the fever there. But ah, was he dreaming... or was there more! Freighted on that fateful breeze was a sound, so faint he could scarcely believe he had heard! It was there... and then it was gone. Music... the fragmented strain from a song. Its extreme tenuity precluded any practical identity, and suggested to him it must have come from a great distance. But not having yet regained the full measure of his extrasensory audient faculty, he could only conjecture.

And so, like a drowning man who clutches at a straw, he grasped and embosomed the hope that fate held out to him. In his present frame of mind, he could only believe it to be a message charging him to renew his faith in a destiny that was drawing near its quickening. When the beauty of reality is unable to enter the heart through the eyes, it gains access through the mind... and in such circumstance one must be content with any blessings received: His grief was gone!

The day drew on, and its warmth cooled into early evening as he sat alone, paging through the voluminous compendium of his ancient past, gleaning for a clue that would facilitate the success of his moiling search. At length the voice of Doctor Richards near at hand broke in upon his reverie. "It's supper time, Colonel," he softly informed him. "Shall we go inside? I've ordered dinner to be catered here, and have reserved a table for later, at the Golden Peacock. I want you to wear your full dress uniform, with all your awards of distinction and honor... everything." He accentuated the end of his speech with a smile of satisfaction and bestowed pride, a gesture whose interpretation was not lost on Kilmeade, for his extra-audient perception had now fully returned to its former state of par excellence... indeed, had far exceeded it! For, when one sense of perception is lost to a man, the predominant remaining sense is multiplied tenfold. It relates to the law of teleology.

"Your thoughtfulness warms my tepid heart, Doctor," his friend responded, returning the man's smile. "You believe it is possible someone will recognize me, and may be of help in finding what I seek. It's certainly worth a try, sir. Let us be off then."

Their trip by taxi was uneventful, although he was aware his heart's rhythm was somewhat accelerated, a phenomenon he readily understood. But when he entered the doorway to the foyer he was suddenly struck with an overwhelming sense of nostalgia, and his heart danced in accompaniment to the bittersweet memories that assailed him. His thoughts became wild with anticipatory visions of the unforgettable beauty of the past, and his steps faltered for an instant! Richards' grasp on his arm tightened, and then relaxed as Kilmeade's hand touched his grip in reassurance. "It's so much the same!" he managed, in a hoarse but subdued whisper. "Too much the same."

His friend nodded, "Yes, I was afraid it might be. Perhaps we had better leave. It was a bad idea... coming here. Just say the word."

"No, I'll stick it out. We've so much to possibly gain. And nothing to lose."

The waiter seated them at a vacant table in the corner of the room, took their order for drinks, and departed... soon returning with glasses and a carafe of vintage wine. "The best in the house!" he assured them. "Welcome back, Major... I should say... Colonel, Kilmeade. It's been a long time."

Kilmeade's heart stirred with welcome excitement. Could Richards' plan be bearing fruit? "Yes, indeed it has... and it's good to be back."

"And Mignonette... How is Mignonette?"

"I really don't know, sir. That was to be my question to you. I had hoped you could tell me. We became separated through the misfortunes of the war. Just before its end I was wounded and shipped back to the States. I am searching for her now! Is there anyone left here who might help me in locating her?"

"I'll ask around, Colonel, and get back to you; but this place is under new management, and I am the only one remaining of the former hired help. She stayed on for a while after the war had ended, but suddenly disappeared one day. I do know she searched everywhere for you, until she left! I supposed she had found you. But I will ask around." He bowed and went back to his chores.

Kilmeade sat in gloomy silence, sipping his now tasteless wine, his thoughts dwelling on that last memorable evening he had spent with Mignonette at this same cafe, and remembering how they had left early, to be alone and give expression to the supernal love that had possessed them... and the incredible nearness they had experienced and shared! Doctor Richards, feeling awkward and helpless, considered it best to leave him to his thoughts.

A few minutes went by, and the orchestra struck up a loud fanfare, and a man approached center stage and addressed the many guests occupying the cafe. "Ladies and gentle, our establishment has the distinction tonight to be honored from out of the past by a celebrated American war hero, who spent many nights enjoying our hospitality. Among many other honors awarded to him for bravery and noble service, our country bestowed upon him its highest medal, the Croix de Guerre. It is said in high places it was primarily due to his distinguished efforts that Paris was saved in those last days of the war. Please welcome Colonel Scott Kilmeade!" As he spoke, a bright spotlight pierced through the dim light of the room to where Kilmeade sat, illuminating him in the span of its glaring brilliance! The entrepreneur, himself had been an officer in the French army, and had heard the substantial rumors of Kilmeade's exploits at the battle of Meaux, and had long entertained a great admiration for him.

Kilmeade arose and acknowledged the enthusiastic and stirring ovation bestowed him, bowing and gesturing in affable response to their homage. With an impulsive motion he swept his wine glass from the table and raised it flamboyantly aloft, as the cheering patrons fell silent. With sincere emotion in his voice he offered an impassioned toast: "To the noble fighting men of France, and the beautiful women for whom they fought! Vive la France!" He placed the glass to his lips and drained its contents, then returned it to the table and modestly resumed his seat. The rousing ovation burst out anew!

Once more, the fanfarade! The entrepreneur raised his arms for silence. "The establishment of the Golden Peacock now offers a specialty number in tribute to the memory of the Colonel and his wartime sweetheart who sang here so beautifully for so many years." He gestured to the orchestra, and withdrew.

And then it came... The music to the song fate had entombed in the darkness of his mind, and that had lain sequestered there, awaiting faithfully to be released once more into the heart of he who loved so well.

Kilmeade sat as though in a trance. The waves of music swept over him and into his soul . . .and tears, at once of happiness and sorrow, sprang from his sightless eyes, and coursed his cheeks. He was grateful for the shielding privacy of his opaque glasses, for he was powerless to stem their flow. Many guests remembered the song and its words, and sang along with the orchestra, most turning toward him as they sang. It was the crowning tribute of appreciation for a gallant hero! "Ah, the French," he thought, "How well they know the price of sacrifice for a great cause." There was not a soul in the place who did not love Kilmeade, at that moment. But what of those without souls? If such is possible. He was about to discover the answer to that.

Seated several tables away were three rough-looking men who seemed engrossed in rather intense conversation, occasionally staring balefully in Kilmeade's direction as though he might be the topic of their discussion. He concentrated his attention on them, and soon learned it was indeed he who they were talking about, and in most derogatory terms, to the point of threatening him with bodily harm. He was convinced they would continue their diatribe and eventually rouse themselves into action, like the ilk of such react who have been indoctrinated in the culture of their animal instincts.

He quietly turned to his oblivious companion and apprised him of the situation, concluding his observations with the instruction: "If they approach and confront me, let me handle the situation. I know how to deal with them!"

Richards frowned. "Do you think that is wise, sir? In the ordinary sense of parity, you are at a great disadvantage." He was a student of medical science, and lacked the adequate toughness and mental assurance characteristic of a military officer.

Kilmeade's smile was easy, and bespoke the immensity of his self-confidence. "There is no consideration as to parity in war. A man must always believe he cannot lose. That is the stuff that victory is made of! I am grateful for your interest regarding my safety... but, trust me, I will win. If it were not so, I would not say it."

As the two Americans spoke together now, the biggest and most evil looking of the three ruffians, the one who had appeared the most agitated during their discussion, flung the remaining contents of liquor in his glass, down his throat to fortify his bravado, and lurched to his feet, glaring at Kilmeade as he swaggered toward the table where the two friends sat. Kilmeade sensed his approach, even before Richards saw him. "The enemy draws near, my friend... as anticipated. Perhaps you would care to order us another round of drinks at the bar... until this confrontation is resolved, and spare yourself any unpleasant involvement. I will understand!"

Richards shook his head, forgetting for the moment that his friend could not see his gesture. "As I once told you, I have cast my lot with you! I will remain!" He was a mild man, but he lacked no courage or loyalty.

The Russian advanced boldly abreast of the chair where Kilmeade sat, his slouching hulk towering over his adversary. In a snarling voice he proclaimed, "I will have a word with you, ugly American."

Kilmeade came agilely to his feet, minimizing any disadvantage of position. "What could you possibly say that would be of any interest to me? I don't know who you are, nor from the looks of you, would I ever care to learn! I detest bad manners fully as much as I do Russian peasants! Or are they synonymous? Remove your odorous presence from my proximity. You are tainting the bouquet of my wine."

The smug expression on the face of the smiling American enraged the hapless Russian, who was no match for Kilmeade when it came to a battle of wits. Even Richards was enjoying the exchange, chuckling to himself, and was doubly glad he had stayed. He was fast learning what remarkable faculties Kilmeade possessed.

The Russian was nearly apoplectic with frustration and rage. Things were not going as he had planned. He was almost shouting now, as he lashed back at his tormentor, "You arrogant, ugly Americans! We Russians will invade your land and impose our elite system of socialistic government on your decadent democracy, and destroy your effete capitalism. You are a decadent nation made up of bullies and cowards. And you and your military officers are the most cowardly of all!" He was breathless and literally foaming as he ended his tirade.

Kilmeade allowed him to finish, the smile still frozen on his placid face. And then he calmly gave answer: "Coward? I don't know that word." He skewed his face into a look of feigned perplexity. "But you, being Russian, should know it full well." His features reformed, assuming his true feeling of repulsion. "You, and your fellow dogs of depravity demonstrated the reality of that during your rape of the women of a defenseless Berlin!" He tossed his head in savage contempt, in accompaniment with a mocking laugh! "I must say, your choice of adversaries was most befitting you. Although I believe you to have been a good deal overmatched." Then his voice took on a deadly tone. "Would you care... would you dare... to essay a passage of arms with a more answerable opponent? A disabled veteran from that great American fighting machine that dragged you meddling peasants along to a victory you neither implemented nor deserved! I aver you would not have so glibly shared in the noble results of so righteous an effort so well meted and so desperately contended, had I been in attendance at its finalization! I would have driven your rag-tag army from the face of this clean earth, and spitted the felon you call Stalin, on a pike! Have I made my position perfectly clear? And would you prefer I kill you where you stand... or would you opt for a duel, to be fought by gentlemen under rules of honor? For your affront will most surely not go unanswered! I will have my satisfaction!"

The Russian's miserable attempt to humiliate his adversary, having become a disaster, forced him to take recourse to violence as his only avenue remaining for rebuttal.

Kilmeade, on guard against any belligerent contingency that his frustrated opponent might adopt, heard the man's movement of attack he had anticipated. Quicker than the eye could follow, Kilmeade caught his hapless adversary's fist in the palm of his powerful hand in a crushing grip, flinging him ignominiously to the floor on his knees. The ruffian gave a cry of pain and surprise and offered no further resistance.

"I will construe your typically craven assault as a

response in the affirmative," Kilmeade assured him. "Very well, a duel it shall indeed be! Doctor Richards, here," Kilmeade nodded toward his friend, "will act as my second, and join you immediately at your table, to discuss conditions. I bid you leave."

The Russian rose clumsily to his feet, with hatred and a promise of death smoldering in the depths of his eyes, but abject humiliation written across his sullen face. "It is done. I will kill you... for your insolence... and for the honor of Russia."

"There is too little of the latter remaining to give you much satisfaction," Kilmeade quietly offered.

The Russian returned to his table and rejoined his companions, followed by Doctor Richards. Kilmeade resumed his seat, smiling placidly through his darkness at the few nearby witnesses he knew must have observed the confrontation, and nonchalantly sipped his wine.

CHAPTER EIGHT
The Duel

Scott Kilmeade was not intrinsically a man of violence. Only by demand of necessity would he initiate and employ any concomitant measure of such extreme degree. However, at the battle of Meaux, in addition to the grievous wound to his head, the caprice of fate was instrumental in disturbing the equilibrium of a basic value that he would eventually have to confront and readjust.

His blood had run high that day, for his expectations were stirred beyond the excitement of routine combat and his usual fervor of dedicated commitment in the obliteration of an evil and unremitting enemy. Completely unsolicited, and with only tenuous permission, he had assumed control over the military strategy the Allied command had previously followed, substituting instead, the conditions of his own personal assessment, predicated on his belief in the extraordinary endowment of clairaudience that he knew would be vitally instrumental in its success. The magnitude of his responsibility augmented his desire for success, and he envisioned victory within his grasp, for he knew he had acted in honor, and with a righteous faith in substantial reality! And then it came... the exploding shell! And his conscious mind was deprived of its rightful reward of a conclusive resolution! Through all the years of intervening darkness, his desire of a just compensation for his earlier labors during the long, traumatizing campaign across the breadth of France, and his hope for the victory that awaited at the merciful end, were denied him, and lay heavily now within his mind, smoldering! For a righteous and awesome sanguinity had transformed him and cried out for indemnity! How bitter, the victory he never knew! How empty, the resurrected life that fate now meted him... too late for love that could not wait. Violence? Ah, yes! There had been violence then... suffered without reward. But this was another day... in another time! Master, he was now, of his own life and the fragments of a meager destiny that yet remained. He would embrace any violence his course demanded, and welcome its wrested fruits! He knew the Russian would die.

Two days had gone by, and the adversaries and seconds stood together now in the early dawn, secluded in a meadow among a heavy growth of trees, recapitulating the terms and procedures to be followed. A man who had identified himself as a member of the Parisian civil law, was speaking: "It is agreed then, whatever the outcome, neither party will take recourse to the law regarding this matter. This passage at arms is being contested to resolve a personal dispute, and at its conclusion all pertinent action will terminate. No further action by either party, legal or physical, shall be considered or taken." He turned his attention directly to the two participants. "Your pistols have each been loaded with a single round. When that shot has been fired, the duel is ended, hit or miss. At the beginning, you will stand back to back, and I will start my count to ten in slow and measured cadence. You will take one step on each count. At my call of ten you can turn and fire at your own discretion. You then have twenty seconds in which to prepare your aim and fire your shot. If, after the elapse of that grace period you have not yet fired, you will have abrogated your opportunity to do so. Have I made this all clear to both of you?"

Kilmeade and the Russian both nodded.

The official then handed each weapon to the seconds for their inspection and approval, and then gave one of the pistols to each contestant, announcing: "Take your positions! And may the grace of God go to the righteous."

The two participants placed themselves in the prescribed position, and awaited the count to begin. The official began his cadence: "One... two..." The antagonists stepped forward, away from one another in rhythm to the cadence, each holding his weapon at the ready. The official's count continued... "eight... nine ... ten!" Both men whirled about, simultaneously! The Russian raised his weapon deliberately, to take aim, just as Kilmeade fired.

The sneer on the Russian's face faded, as his head snapped back from the impact of the American's bullet! A tiny red spot appeared in the middle of his forehead, and his eyes glazed over as he sank silently to his knees in the grassy meadow and toppled forward on his lifeless face.

Kilmeade turned in the direction where Doctor Richards was standing, and spoke, "God's will be done. This shall give some redress to the women of Berlin, for their chastity that he and his barbarous ilk defiled! And the world is well rid of one more disciple of Satan."

The official shook his head in amazement at Kilmeade's skill and aplomb, and then remarked, "It's quite a sight to see two brave men risk death for an ideal they believed in so strongly... but sad that one of them must die."

But Kilmeade would give no quarter to an untruth, not even to favor obeisance to the dead. "Brave? I think not. The only thing he believed in was that I am blind! He could not conceive that he would lose. His arrogance swaggered with him into hell."

"I cannot believe that you could be blind and still shoot with such accuracy," the man marveled.

"Believe what you wish, my good man. But since the point has been brought up, I will tell you that my audio-sensory perception, particular to me, can access sounds beyond the reach of human sensibility, either visual or auditory, and that tell me truths you would not believe... pictorial images more truly visualized within my mind than those normally seen by the human eye. If you can believe what you have just witnessed, you can better understand what I have just told you." He paused, and a look of sadness came across his face as he continued. "But I would gladly trade this gift from God for the sight of just one remembered scene of a world rich with all its beauty that once caressed these futile eyes of mine." He gave an expostulatory grimace as he turned away.

As they were leaving, Doctor Richards approached the official and handed him a small, sealed envelope. "Sir, he said, "This is for your much appreciated services. It is Colonel Kilmeade's way of expressing his gratitude for your understanding commitment to a just cause, and for an enterprise professionally executed. Go with God." Smiling, the official shook Richards' extended hand, bowed and departed.

Richards joined Kilmeade, and together they walked from the scene of conflict... Richards with a sensation of deep and abiding relief, and Kilmeade entertaining a strange but fulfilling emotion of satisfaction that he never thought to question, for he believed the consequence of his victory was justified: At the risk of his own life, he had confronted and destroyed an evil adversary! It was but a continuation of the war against oppression he had waged for so many years. In the calendar of his existence, it was only yesterday that he had been engaged in a life and death campaign dedicated to that same purpose. The time that lay between was lost in the residual of his memory. His psyche was inculcated by the traumatic impact that justifiable and expedient violence had so indelibly engraved there! That is not to say Kilmeade had lost his good judgment or any awareness of the difference between right and wrong, for that would be madness, an affliction that flourishes in the vacuum of weakness. His greatest strength lay in his mental toughness, an asset that was his greatest pride! It was simply the distortion of time that now played such an integral role in the irregularity of his values. Its effect on him was similar to that of the circadian principal, which is induced by jet lag. The clock in his brain was ticking to the cadence of the battle of Meaux.

CHAPTER NINE
Ships That Pass

When the two men returned to their inn, they found a message awaiting them. It was the eagerly anticipated answer to their request for an appointment with the highly accredited surgeon in Switzerland. There was a personal note added at the bottom, and written by educated hand, explaining the priority of attention given to Kilmeade's application: "My establishment extends special consideration to all wounded personnel of the late war. I look forward to serving you at your earliest convenience." It was signed, H. Vandermeer.

Richards read the note aloud to his charge, exclaiming his approval. "It's been a most fortuitous day. Lady Luck is finally smiling on your hopes and efforts! I have a good feeling that this is at last the beginning event in the resurrection and fulfillment of your life."

Kilmeade smiled through his repugnant darkness in response to his friend's optimistic enthusiasm, with something like hope rising in his heart. Just one more step taken in the right direction, he thought. But he remained silent. He was thinking of his lost Mignonette, and not of his blindness. His hope was stirred by the prospect that his recovered sight would more positively facilitate and thus hasten his reunion with his beloved, not with the return of sight itself. But his consummate ideal was to be able to gaze fondly once more upon the exquisite beauty of the creature who had given him the desire to live... and his happiness! He must have it all... Or he would take nothing.

It was some two hundred and sixty miles from Paris

to the town of Lausanne, a day's journey, and they began to prepare for the trip immediately. First, Richards arranged by phone for lodging at a conveniently located hotel in that area, and then sent a wire notifying the hospital of their arrival time. This taken care of, the two men went to Kilmeade's bank and withdrew traveling money. It was the same bank in which he had deposited money for Mignonette years earlier, and into which, before leaving for France, Richards had transferred a reasonable amount of funds for expense purposes.

Immediately upon regaining his memory, several weeks earlier, Kilmeade had contacted this bank, hoping to obtain information regarding Mignonette's present location; but was told she had withdrawn her entire account, and had disappeared without leaving a referable address. The bank official did say that she had told him she was relocating to another country. At the time, Kilmeade had wondered if she had meant America. Had she gone there in search for him? But, after considering the possibility, he discarded the idea. He felt sure she would remain close to Paris, for hadn't he told her that if he lived he would come to her. And hadn't she promised to sing their song, so that he could hear and know she still loved and was waiting. No, she would keep her sacred promise... Of that he was sure. And so now he felt more sure than ever that he would soon find her! How barren the world without beauty and love! How empty the soul without loyalty and hope!

Early the following day Scott Kilmeade and his man, Richards, arrived at Gare de Paris, where they purchased tickets and checked their baggage through to their destination. There was a short wait for the arrival of their scheduled train from the west, so they decided to pass the interval in the refreshment lounge.

Like so many soldiers during the stress of the late war, Kilmeade had acquired the custom of indulging in a drink or two as an anodyne for pain, or to relieve the trifling monotony of an idle interlude. Although he had not drunk hard liquor for five years, the familiar habit had accompanied the return of his memory, for his mental clock was ticking in the realm of the past, and his blindness only made his adjustment to the present more difficult. Reality is the knowledge which your dominate senses have obtained through experience, and that your subsequent thought process has accepted as existent; unlike the strange, suffocatingly invisible world into whose circumscribed precincts he had summarily awakened.

They settled into a booth, and Kilmeade ordered a double shot of rum and coke in a tall glass. His companion opted for a glass of vintage wine. The waitress, a pretty, young girl of perhaps sixteen, eyed the handsome officer and his impressive military uniform resplendent with insignia of valor.

She beamed him a gracious smile, and with effusive admiration induced by her considerable youth, expressed her thoughts in limited and unfamiliar English, "You must be Colonel Scott Kilmeade," she exulted. "All of France will be forever grateful to you for what you have done for us. I am so happy to meet you in person and thank you." Her voice then took on a more sober tone, tinged with a note of commiseration that bordered on sadness. "We were told, God forbid! That you had been a casualty of war." She offered her hand as an added expression of sincerity.

Kilmeade, unaware of her gesture, gave no response

for a moment. Richards, to salvage the situation decorously, put a finger to his eyes, and frowning, shook his head.

Quickly interpreting the situation, the waitress grasped Kilmeade's hand where it lay atop the table, and pressed it to her lips. There were tears in her eyes . . .and her voice, as she managed a word of sympathy, "I am so terribly sorry! Great deeds sometimes require great sacrifice! Only God can give you a fitting reward ... a special place in Heaven!"

Kilmeade, aware of what was transpiring, lightly replied, "I might be considered somewhat of a casualty, I suppose, but we are on our way to Switzerland today, to see a surgeon who may perhaps be able to give me back my sight. I have my fingers crossed."

"And you have my prayers... and those of all France, too, I am sure!" she responded. She curtsied and went to fetch their order.

They sat for a short while drinking and conversing, and then the announcement that their Express had arrived, came over the loudspeaker system, and they made preparation to leave. Kilmeade stood up and reached into his pocket, bringing forth a small handful of loose change, which he placed on the table as a generous tip for the waitress in expression of his appreciation for the sensitivity and profusion of her kind words. As he did so, a small, good luck charm he always carried, inadvertently disengaged itself from the collected mass of coins and fell unnoticed to the floor.

As they boarded the train, Richards glanced at his wristwatch. "Twelve twenty," he announced. "Right on time. We should reach our destination in about six hours." He was a punctual man, and gave proper attention to detail... an important characteristic that

Kilmeade had always appreciated in any man. The span of life was composed of details... many that were important; and to a military officer, some were vital. How well he knew that.

The trip was uneventful, and Kilmeade dozed intermittently. Traveling was always lulling and restful to him. Twenty minutes out of Paris, he was awakened by the rushing sound of another train as it passed them coming in from the east. "The Special from Lausanne," he heard Richards say. He nodded acquiescently, and idly noted the nostalgic sound as it thundered past and faded away into the distance. Life was like that, he thought. Sound and fury, and then gone! He dozed off again.

A little after six o'clock their train pulled into the Lausanne depot. The sun was low and red in the west, and the air was cool from the added elevation. They claimed their baggage, and as they were arranging for transportation a man approached them and introduced himself. "Messieurs, je vous demande pardon! Je suisle chauffeur de hospitalier." He paused, searching his vocabulary for the appropriate expression in English. "You are going to the hospital, n'est pas?"

Kilmeade smiled warmly. "Oui, c'est vrai."

"Come. I will take you. Le docteur, Hans Vandermeer, has sent me."

"Well, that's what I call service," Kilmeade said to Richards. "I hope he's as good a doctor as he is a host."

"He has a reputation as the best," Richards replied.

The chauffeur joined in the accolade, "He is the best, mes messieurs... as a docteur, and as a man! You will see."

They loaded into the hospital van, man and baggage, and were on their way to the end of their journey, some sixteen kilometers deeper into the elevated panorama of Switzerland.

Doctor Richards' first view of the sanitarium left him with an indelibly favorable impression. And the more he increasingly saw as their sojourn extended, the more his admiration grew. The size of the facility was more than twice as large as it had been five years earlier, when Mignonette had been a patient there. The considerable monies his services had garnered, the good surgeon had continually invested into improving every aspect devoted to modern medicine and into acquiring the technical equipment demanded by his advanced methods. His success in dealing with the incurable had become legend! And the techniques he employed in the practice of his specialty, the treatment of brain damage, whether caused by disease or injury, were unknown to modern medical science. Many eminent doctors throughout the world came to study his methods and procedures of advanced surgery. His efforts too, were brilliant and tireless. He labored like a man driven in pursuit of a great crusade. Those who were wealthy paid in full for his services; but those who were financially unable to afford his stipend, paid very little or nothing. That he accepted any remuneration at all, he was once heard to say, was to purchase the needed equipment and supplies, and to pay his hired help and the few associate doctors who complemented his staff.

Their chauffeur escorted them into a plush waiting room and introduced them to the receptionist, and then departed. The receptionist informed them that the doctor was supervising an operation at the moment, and then called to inform him his expected guests had arrived. "He won't be long," she told them. "He's been quite intrigued by your case. He has anticipated meeting you ever since you contacted him. He enjoys a challenge, and thinks your unique condition will be the ultimate test of his skills." She smiled, "If anyone can help you, I'm sure he will." It was obvious this woman held Doctor Vandermeer and his professional ability in highest esteem. "I've seen him do the impossible so many times."

Warming to the subject of her employer's remarkable prowess, as well as hoping to fortify Kilmeade's faith in the probability of success in his operation, she continued her accolade. "They still tell the story about the young woman whose life he saved... and the life of her premature child... about five years ago. It was just after I came here. Except for him, those two would not have survived! Believe me! I was there!" Her eyes grew wide at the vivid recollection! "His attentive care and dedication pulled them through." She shook her head in puzzlement, "And to top it all off, he refused to take any money for his services. I never could understand why... She was really quite wealthy." She paused for a moment, and then concluded, "I could go on like this for hours... there are so many. He's a great man... with a great heart."

The phone rang and the receptionist answered, listening for a moment, and then replying, "Thank you, Doctor," she hung up. "He will be here shortly. He's washing up." She smiled, "He says not to leave."

Kilmeade noted the smile in her voice, and answered with his own. "I've nowhere to go. I've already been everywhere... and everywhere is always just the same to me." He had not met the man yet, but found himself pleased with his attentiveness and courtesy. He certainly was unusual. What was said about him must have some semblance of truth, else why the extravagant endorsement from all those who knew him. For the first time, he felt optimistic about his chances of reclaiming his sight.

And then he heard the door to the waiting room open, and felt the presence of the man as he entered, and heard his quiet and reassuring voice as he spoke his greeting. And a sudden sensation, incomprehensible and disturbing swept into his mind, confusing his senses. It was there, and then it was gone... a hodgepodge message that told him nothing... because it said too much, and too quickly!

Kilmeade stood up and reached for the handclasp he knew was there. The doctor's hand was warm and friendly. You had to like a man who shook hands that way. "It's nice to finally meet you," was all he said.

"I hope we can be of mutual service to each other," the doctor replied. "Your case is a very interesting one. I hope to prove much in the process of treating you. I have waited a long time for this opportunity... much longer than you have waited to be treated. The difference being, because of the circumstances, your wait was harder to endure. But we shall soon remedy that, God willing!" He motioned to Richards, "Bring your friend, and come with me. I will show you where he will be staying for the next several weeks. You may stay here, too, if you wish. We have ample accommodations."

"Thank you, sir," Dr. Richards replied. "I have reserved lodging at a nearby inn, but perhaps it would be best if I stay close to him until after the initial surgery is completed. He has grown to accept my assistance and rely on my understanding to a considerable extent, and frankly, I think I need him as much as he needs me." He smiled gratefully as he concluded, "I assure you that both of us appreciate your kindness and consideration. It has become apparent to me `why' you have been so successful with what you have been doing here, for I have been witnessing the `how.'"

He led them some distance along a deep-carpeted corridor, and stopping at a door, opened it and stepped inside. His guests followed him in. "This will be your home as long as you are here," Dr. Vandermeer announced. "It is the best we have, and accommodates two persons. Dr. Richards can familiarize you with the interior facilities. You will find there is everything here you will need for comfortable living. Have yourself a restful sleep tonight, Colonel Kilmeade. We start your intensive examination early in the morning." He turned to go, and then stopped. "Forgive me," he said, "I almost forgot... an attendant will be here shortly, with a menu. You can order what you like, for dinner. We have quite an elaborate kitchen at the disposal of our guests... enjoy." He smiled, then bowed and took his leave, closing the door behind him.

* * *

That same day, back in Paris, a train pulled into the station, and among those disembarking, was a beautiful young woman tightly clasping the tiny hand of a beautiful four-year-old boy with hair as golden as his mother's. It was exactly one o'clock in the afternoon. She addressed the porter beside her, carrying her luggage, "Will you kindly call me a taxi? We will be in the refreshment lounge. Ask for Francois, and tell him it's for Mademoiselle Lescaut, and I have a lot of shopping to do." She gave him a generous tip. They continued on, and once inside, they seated themselves in a booth and ordered soft drinks from the pretty young waitress.

They were just finishing their drinks when Francois showed up. Leaving a tip, they hurried to the taxi and were soon on their way to the fashionable shopping district of Paris. As they rode along, the child's mother noticed he was engrossed with a bright object he held in his hand. "What have you there, Scotty?" she asked him.

"This," he replied, holding it out to her in his open palm. "I found it under the table in the sweet shop. It's pretty!" He handed it to her. "May I keep it?" He looked at her hopefully. "Please! I like it!"

She held it in her hand, examining it closely. "It is pretty!" she agreed. "Yes, my darling, of course you may keep it." She placed it back into his tiny, eager hand. She was thinking: "It's not expensive enough to trouble finding the owner and returning it." And besides, she took special delight in fostering his pleasure. This wee child was her dominant happiness and the major focus of her existence... the precious and only viable remaining fragment of an ill-fated love! Which is to say, he was the preponderant essence of reality that life had endowed to her!

The object in question was a miniature replica of a soldier's dog tag, about an inch and a half in length, cast in silver. And enameled on its shiny surface was an American flag, and underneath was the date and inscription, Normandy, 1944!

CHAPTER TEN
The Mills of the Gods

A few weeks after Mignonette's misadventure on horseback and her subsequent sojourn in the hospital for the birth of her child, she had fully recovered her normal health and strength, and the newly adopted pattern of her life continued for a short interval uneventful and undisturbed. All of her waking hours were intensely devoted to the maternal responsibilities this precious new mite of life demanded of her. And all of these waking hours she thanked God and rejoiced that He had allotted her this sacred benefaction, whose creation, the man she loved had shared with her.

Several times she had ventured to the nearby city of Lausanne accompanied by her nurse and handmaid, Susan Johnson. It was a welcome reprieve from the rigorous routine of dedicated attention her duties of motherhood necessitated. On one particular occasion, as they were having lunch in one of the more frequently patronized cafes, a woman from among a group sitting in a booth across from them, took notice of the infant cradled in Mignonette's arms, and ventured a compliment, accompanied by a beaming smile, "Oh, what a beautiful baby!" And then added, "It must be a girl... She's too pretty to be a boy... and so tiny!"

Mignonette, evincing a proud mother's delight, beamed the woman a grateful smile in return for the flattering observation, and replied, "As a matter of fact, Scotty is a boy... and handsome, like his father. He is so tiny because of premature birth. But I know he will grow to be big and strong... like his father was." The terminal phrase of her remark, though she tried to maintain the same spirited tone to its finality... and hoping she had succeeded, nevertheless carried a tinge of sadness.

The inflection of her voice, and the tense of the verb that she employed, however, were too obvious to be disregarded, and the woman's reply was carefully expressed in respectful sympathy. "His father was a soldier, then? How dreadfully sad and unfortunate! I am so terribly sorry." She shook her head sadly to accentuate the impact of her words.

And then, to change the subject, the memory of which she felt must be painful to Mignonette, she inquired as to the identity of the person who had been the doctor at her child's birth, realizing there must have been complications attendant to a premature child. "It wouldn't possibly have been Dr. Vandermeer, would it? The recently relocated surgeon on the hill above town?"

Mignonette was a little surprised, not realizing the doctor was so well known. "Why, yes, it was he... and a remarkably fine doctor he was, indeed! He saved my baby, and me too, I believe."

"I'm not at all surprised," the woman continued. "He saved my husband's life a couple of months ago... after the terrible accident he had. And his fee was exceptionally reasonable. He only charges what his patients can well afford." It was obvious, for good reason, that she thought highly of the doctor's character and kindness as well as his unusual technical expertise.

Later, when her group got up to leave, she thoughtfully expressed her good wishes, "It's been nice talking to you. I hope you and your lovely little boy enjoy a long and happy life, and that your troubles are all behind you. Goodbye."

Mignonette was impressed. "Thank you for your

kind words and wishes. I hope your husband completely recovers soon. Goodbye."

Several days after this experience, Mignonette, by course of natural procedure sent her nurse to the hospital to learn the amount of money she owed for her treatment there. Her nurse came back with the information there was no charge. She was told by the receptionist that the doctor charged no fee for emergency treatment resulting from traumatic injuries caused by accidents of a violent or unfortunate nature.

Mignonette pondered this bit of surprising information for some time, before finally deciding to confront its source in person and set the controversy in her mind at rest. Her inability to accept the message's content as compatible with the candid and unsolicited information she had received in town, made it quite reasonably unbelievable without further explanation, and raised an incomprehensible but disturbing thought in her mind that left her feeling vulnerable and insecure. There was more here than had been stated, and its ambiguity demanded exploration. Little did she anticipate the incredible and explosive revelation the culmination of that effort would eventually engender! She remained adamant in her conviction of one thing: There was an intriguing mystery here that piqued her interest, challenged her imagination, and cried out loudly for investigation. She was not intransigent in regard to accepting reasonable favors, but she was adamant in her commitment to paying for honorable and critical services rendered her, whether they were solicited or not.

In conformance with her wish to keep the issue in low profile and thus obviate the possibility of precipitating an unpleasant confrontation, she decided to wait, and speak of it casually at her baby's next scheduled checkup several days hence.

And so, on this particular autumn morning, seated in the tonneau of her town car with little Scotty in a bassinet beside her, she was driven to the hospital by her chauffeur and handyman. Upon arrival, her chauffeur accompanied her into the waiting room, carrying the bassinet.

Nurse Shumacher smiled an affable greeting as Mignonette and her entourage approached, and together the two women, with the nurse carrying the baby and bassinet, entered a private examination cubicle, while the chauffeur remained in the outer reception room.

After the usual routine questions had been asked and answered, and the baby's weight had been checked, the nurse announced in an admiring tone that everything was going splendidly. "Our little Scotty is the perfect picture of robust health. He has gained two pounds, and is becoming such a beautiful little child." And then added, in a more sober tone, "Considering the adverse circumstances surrounding his birth, you have both been most remarkably blessed!"

It was comforting and encouraging information given to an understandably apprehensive woman so peremptorily inaugurated to motherhood, and Mignonette's reaction was responsive to her relief and appreciation. "I am inestimably grateful for what you and the doctor have done for me and my precious child! I must tell you I shall be forever indebted for your heroic service! And I must insist on paying the Doctor's usual fee for those services. It will be no hardship to me. I have ample wealth. And I am sure the doctor can put his well-earned fee to good use." Her tone brooked no refusal. "Please have him make out my bill as soon as possible. I will feel so much better. It's really the only substantial way I have of acknowledging the high esteem in which I hold his skill and dedication as a physician and his understanding and empathy for the misfortune of a fellow human being."

The nurse was left with no recourse but to accede to such a sincere and forthright plea. "I will apprise him of what you have said, and how you feel. I'm sure he will listen and understand. You can expect to receive your statement of account by post in a day or so. And unless there is a problem sooner, I'll see you in two weeks for your and Scotty's final examinations. Goodbye, Mignonette, until then, and God bless."

Several days later she received her hospital statement of account by post, as promised, and upon opening it was relieved to find it to be clearly itemized and understandable. She began to realize she had given her imagination too much latitude. Surely there was no mystery here. The man had only wished to camouflage a gesture of kindness to what he saw as a disadvantaged and vulnerable woman in her time of distress, by implementing a too obvious subterfuge by way of justification. He could easily be forgiven for that... and she reprimanded herself for not realizing the truth sooner and thus accepting his kindness with unjaundiced vision. Even as she made note that she would, at their next meeting, offer an explanation by way of contrition, she realized it was the prevailing influence of Scott Kilmeade that had induced the earlier reaction. Hadn't he always said, as a preamble to his belief that a man should insist upon moral control of the direction of his own life: "Implicitly trust no one, and always question the motives of others, as well as your own!" The timely recollection of this bit of forensic wisdom restored some measure of her self-assurance and a feeling of justification, serving to warm his memory in her heart, as thoughts of him always did.

And so, as she sat at the table in her garden on this late autumn day, intermittently rocking baby Scotty in the bassinet at her feet, she immediately made out a draft on her Swiss bank for the full amount, accompanied by a heartfelt note of gratitude, and addressed to the hospital.

While engaged in writing the note, she suddenly decided, as a gesture of friendship and appreciation, to arrange an informal luncheon at her home for the doctor and any members of his staff that wished to attend. She left the specific date open, to be selected later for a time convenient to them. She had lately been thinking of resuming the interrupted pattern of her life and gradually becoming involved in the local social activities that availed. A reclusive life did not complement her nature, and she wished her son to be advantaged within a normal environment. She reasoned that a moderate degree of such indulgence could not interfere with her vigil of devotion to her errant lover, although occasionally she missed the thrill of satisfaction she had enjoyed for so long as the lionized vocalist at the Golden Peacock. Also, her state of motherhood precluded any thought of her accepting a binding commitment as a public entertainer, had she been so inclined.

And so, with her letter completed and its contents sealed inside, she placed it on her writing table for her handyman to post later that day. And then, with a sigh of some satisfaction, she succumbed to a feeling of relief for a nettlesome trifle finally and aptly dispatched, and sank back in her chair, letting her eyes stray appreciatively about and among the collective verdure of her beautifully created garden. All was going reasonably well again, and she felt her Love would be coming to her soon! God was in His Heaven! Patience was her forte.

The sky above stretched clear and blue across the heavens. The leaves of the fabled apple tree, under whose sheltering branches she now sat, still clung staunchly, in loyal obeisance to the waning season, but gradually, through the passing days their defecting comrades had begun to carpet the ground underneath. High on a branch, half hidden from sight below, a small, brown bird was singing a belated farewell to summer. In defiance of her momentary optimism, Mignonette's heart impulsively beat time with the tempo of its sadness... and her voice, capitulating, broke softly into song! A cold wind gusted the blanket around the infant in its nest at her feet, and he began to cry! While seven thousand miles away, oblivious of time and season, bereft of sight and sound, a man lay silent in untouchable space.

And then the siege of an incredible Alpine winter thrust its icy austerity disruptively across the fated loneliness of her life, harsh and implacable! Two days after her letter was posted, the snow began to fall and continued uninterrupted for five days. There was hardly time to stock up on food and supplies. And the cold was unbearable. Lake Geneva was a block of ice. To a person of thoughtful inclination, it might reasonably appear as if it were nature's method of punishment, in retaliation for the callous years of devastation it had suffered under the evil machinations of an unconscionable mankind.

Sometime during that long winter a formal letter had come to Mignonette in response to her invitation, explaining the obvious necessity for delaying any such commitment until the weather had improved... possibly in early spring, and expressing the staff's appreciation for Mignonette's gesture of thoughtfulness and congeniality. It was signed by nurse Shumacher.

And so, as the months of that deadly winter dragged slowly along, the young mother directed the focus of her attention to the loving care of her precious charge. No child was ever sheltered more securely from the threatening danger of such pernicious elements as these that held them captive. So intense was her dedication to the welfare of her child, she became oblivious to the onerous obstinance of time; advantaging it instead as a blessing that had peremptorily initiated an intimate and vital exchange of affection in the process of their incipient relationship. The child had instinctively sensed his mother's increased attention as dependency on his affection, and had in turn given complementary response. And so a great rapport was equitably established: The impulse of each to be needed satisfying the desire of the other to gratify that need! And so, for the punishing length of that awful winter, mother and child clung close and secure with a rapport that no disruptive influence could diminished.

For a while she fretted about the fate of her beloved apple tree. Surely it could not survive the killing frost that held its icy domain in bondage! It had been displaced from the much milder region of southern France, and such unanticipated harshness of an inordinate Alpine winter was a real and mortal threat. And then a thought came to her... not too unusual, considering her cast of mind: This tree was a symbol of her romantic ideal. And, like that ideal, it was engulfed in an unequal struggle against a great and sinister force. Whatever fate the tree would suffer, to falter or endure, would be an omen to their love! This strange belief was but an added icon, a desperate hope that bolstered her resolve to cling yet to the enduring faith that her precious love would one day return to her! If the tree should die, then her hope would die with it!

For a while, upon first arising each fateful morning of that long and punishing winter, she would gaze through the window, out into the garden where the apple tree stood, and for long and excruciating moments, study the details of its stalwart silhouette that reared in noble and majestic defiance against the rigors of its ordeal, searching for any infinitesimal evidence that the tree still lived. But the tree stood adamant and taciturn, yielding up no encouraging sign. And, each time, her heart would anguish a little, and she would turn impatiently away from the window and begin to sing her lover's favorite song, the manta of the apple tree. And her tiny child, wherever he was, in his crib or nestled in her arms, would smile happily and coo along with her.

There was another game she played to fortify her hope that she would eventually reclaim her happiness... a drowning person grasps at straws: "If a robin alights and sings from a branch of the tree before the first day of spring," she told herself. "He will come."

In this finite world that God, in His generosity created for the happiness of man, every beginning must come to an end: And so spring drew ever nearer each day, and Mignonette had gradually relinquished her daily routine of gazing from her window into the garden, searching for any sign of continued life in the tree. She had eventually convinced herself that it surely remained! And so she patiently awaited the dawn of the last day of winter, hoping to learn the final answer then.

On the eve of that last day she had gone to bed early, hoping to get a good night's rest to fortify herself for the momentous revelation the morrow would bring... so strong was her belief in the supposition of her self-created omen! But her mind was too beset with anxiety and anticipation to permit the relaxation she sought.

It was several hours before she finally fell into a fitful and troubled sleep harassed by wild and portentous dreams: She sat detached and alone on a hillside, an unwilling spectator of a great battle that raged in the near distance in front of her. Her ears were assailed by the punishing cacophony of the machines of war. The sky was dark with aircraft overhead, their guns spitting death on the fighting men below. The sound of tanks and artillery cannon thundered and blazed among the ranks of struggling men, muffling their dying screams. And then her eyes were caught and held in hypnotic focus on the nearer foreground where the solitary figure of a dynamic warrior stood in isolated splendor, desperately urging his men on to greater feats of courage and valor, himself a tower of strength and courage! If ever a man were in the dire position of harm's way, and remained oblivious of his peril, it was most certainly he! And then, with a terrible shock, she suddenly and unmistakably became aware of his identity: Scott Kilmeade, her beloved passion! Who else could it have been! A dream is the child born of the dreamer's mind, and this man was her hero... her god! The awful reality burst into her brain like an exploding shell and she awake in anguish, bathed in morbid perspiration, sobbing uncontrollably.

The sun was high in the sky and the air seemed unseasonably warm for a winter day. She remained momentarily so shaken by her prophetic dream she had forgotten this was the last day of winter. Tomorrow it would be spring! And then she remembered her omen and he test regarding the tree and the robin, and her heart lost any hope that it would be fulfilled.

She was roused from her thoughts by sounds of discomfort from the crib beside her bed, and feeling a bit guilty of selfishness and neglect, she hastily arose and attended the needs of her helpless charge, for the moment dismissing her own problems from immediate consideration. It was all foolishness anyway, she told herself.

A little later, as she sat in the rocker near the window that overlooked the garden at the rear of the house, and while holding her baby in her arms and softly crooning a lullaby, she suddenly became aware of a beautiful sound she had not heard for a long, long time: the happy twittering of a bird! She arose quickly, her heart beating hopefully again, and for the first time in a week, gazed out through the window once more, into the garden where the tree stood. What she beheld filled her with momentary delight and then a feeling of incredible awe! On a high branch two red-breasted robins sat close together, conversing in the unmistakable language of springtime. And then the slightly larger of the two suddenly flung his head backward, stretched his neck upward and began pouring out his heart in a beautiful song. The other listened, enthralled... as also did Mignonette. On a small branch just above where the two sat, a spark of color, contrasting to the drab gray of its surroundings, caught her roving eye, and she gazed in fascination and disbelief. It was a tiny, green sprig, the incontrovertible testament to a living tree.

CHAPTER ELEVEN
Revelation

(Part One)

Memory of the winter of 1945-46 would linger for a while in the minds of those who had suffered its severity, but the warm spring following close behind would remain indelibly implanted in the memory of a select few, for beauty is endowed with a substance unrivalled by hardship and pain. Man has a natural inclination to retain that which is dear to him, and a wise man does not strive against nature.

Mignonette spent much of her hours during the day in the flourishing precincts of her garden, accompanied by happy little Scotty, who was now six months old and growing bigger each day. The days were warm with Alpine sunshine and fresh air, and there was no evidence remaining to indicate he had been of immature birth. Never did a child have a more attentive mother. Always she was close by, to serve his needs. He was everything that was good remaining in life for her... Although her heart staunchly clung to the hope that his father would return to her one day, and bring her ideal of true happiness to fruition.

Her garden was rife with early spring blossoms, tulips and daffodils, which she attended daily. And by the middle of April the branches of the apple tree were covered with a thick mantle of lush, green leaves and incipient blossoms. And with thoughts of her lover always in her mind, she would smile and tell herself, "If he comes by autumn, I will bake him and Baby Scotty an apple pie. And we three will sit together in our garden and eat it under our apple tree." And then she would weep a little, dry her tears and bravely continue with her daily chores.

One day, about that time, Mignonette had a visitor. Nurse Shumacher stopped by on her way back from town. There was no trace of winter lingering in the lowlands. Only the eternal snow on the towering Alpine peaks gave evidence to remind of the awesome winter. A gentle breeze rippled the placid, azure surface of Lake Geneva. "She's in the garden with the little boy," Nurse Johnson told her. "At the rear of the house. She will be glad to see you. It's been lonely around here for too long."

"It's been a long winter for everyone," Shumacher replied. "How is she, and the boy?"

"Her physical health is quite good, but I can't say much for her spirits. She lives on hope, I think!" And then she added, as an afterthought, "Little Scotty is just fine. I don't know what she would do without him!" She shook her head sadly. "Life is like that: You win some and lose some."

As Shumacher approached the garden entrance she became aware of a beautiful sound. It was a woman's voice singing an American song that had been popular during the war years. She had heard it sparingly before, sung in the German language, for songs of love are universal. But never had she heard it sung so beautifully and with such depth of emotion! And although the words of the libretto were expressed in the contemporaneous style of the light, romantic popular love song, the vibrant overtones of the singer's voice carried a real and unmistakable message of everlasting devotion and the passion of heartache and broken dreams! Its impact was so overpowering, the inadvertent listener hesitated and thought to turn away, lest her unwelcome intrusion into so private and sensitive a moment might embarrass or offend the singer. But Mignonette caught sight of her visitor immediately and beckoned her to approach, as she finished the last few bars of the song.

"Welcome, my friend, it is so good to see you!" Mignonette spoke with sincere enthusiasm, her demeanor unabashed by Nurse Shumacher's unexpected interruption that had seemingly caught her off guard. For indeed, her song was a sacred invocation in appeal to her lover, and was, in her mind, inculpable of disapproval or denigration. Those who have loved and lost, if they endure, are elevated to a more ascendant plateau in the moral scale of human attainment. Its reward is an endowment of courage that prevails against the threat of death or defeat. True love is beyond fear! It is a glory independent within itself... a monument to anything noble that ever was, and to everything that will ever come to be!

Nurse Shumacher was impressed by Mignonette's composure and invulnerability to any awkward, reactionary embarrassment to the situation, for she knew the circumstances surrounding the woman's celibacy. "I trust I'm not imposing on your solitude, but I was concerned about you and Scotty. I thought it was time I looked in on you... with this long period of severe weather, and all." Then smiling, said, "You and your baby never did have that final check-up." She had thankfully regained her own composure by now... reflecting the disposition of the other woman. "And I also had in mind your invitation to that delightful garden party I have for so long anticipated enjoying.

Life can get pretty dull sometimes, doing the same routine work every day."

"Don't I know it," Mignonette exclaimed in agreement. "And I'm so glad you remembered. Anytime will be fine. Just let me know a few days in advance, as I'll need to arrange for a caterer. And give me an idea then, how many will be coming. The more, the merrier." She laughed.

Nurse Johnson prepared tea and joined the other two in the garden, where they visited together for perhaps an hour. The baby cooed and listened to their chatter, enjoying the conversation and conviviality fully as well as the ladies.

"Your child is a remarkably happy baby," Nurse Shumacher remarked during a lull in the conversation. "Doesn't he ever fuss or cry?"

"Only when he gets hungry, or is uncomfortable," Mignonette replied.

"Don't all men do that," Nurse Shumacher observed, laughing. "God bless them!" They all sighed quietly, in acquiescence.

"Speaking of men," said Mignonette, "Will Doctor Vandermeer be attending our get-together? Make it a point to him, that his company is very much desired, will you?"

"I'm sure the Doctor will be happy to attend," the nurse replied. "But I'll give him your message... and what man will refuse to grant a beautiful woman a request so forthrightly extended?" The accolade drew a smile and a blush from Mignonette in modest response.

They chatted a while longer... small talk, such as the unusual severity of the past winter, the timely rescue a glorious spring had brought, and the friendliness of the townspeople; and then the guest took her leave, with the promise to get back to Mignonette shortly, with a firm date for the party, and the approximate number of guests who would likely attend.

The days went dancing by, and the warm spring weather extended its embrace around the precincts of the Alpine countryside. Most of Mignonette's time was spent in her garden, laboring with dedicated enthusiasm to enhance its charm in preparation for the social gathering she had anticipated for so long. She was justifiably proud of the artistic edifice her devotion to an ideal had so painstakingly created, and the romantic history that lay behind its inspiration! Most who knew her were acquainted with the story of her ill-fated romance with the hero of the decisive battle that had saved the fate of France, and they would sympathize and understand the magnitude of her efforts of commemoration, as well as the intrinsic beauty of the offering itself.

And then, one day, as she was working among the flowers and lush herbage of her garden, she was pleasantly surprised by the appearance of an unexpected but welcome visitor, a tall and distinguished looking gentleman sporting an elegant black beard and debonair moustache.

He approached her and introduced himself. "I am Doctor Vandermeer." His voice was tinged with a tenseness that could have been taken as professionalism, but was predominately kind and pleasantly melodious. "Forgive me for disadvantaging you for so long... I, who know you so well, and you who know me not at all except through reputation." His eyes pierced into her face, as though searching for an expression he hoped not to find, and not finding it, a nuance akin to reprieve tracing into their depth. "That is often the case between doctor and patient, unfortunately, "he continued, "but seemingly unavoidable." The tension in his demeanor had evaporated.

Mignonette beamed him an appreciative smile. "I am glad to meet and identify with you at last. One does not often enjoy the unique reward of being rescued from death by a perfect stranger." She paused to gather her thoughts, overcome by the emotion of an overwhelming gratitude. "My life is a mere triviality compared to the life of my child you also saved... a life more precious to me than my own! I shall forever be in your debt!" Tears that gave evidence of the depth of her emotion and proof of her sincerity welled up in her beautiful eyes. "I have wanted to tell you this for so long a time! I am happy I can at last express my gratitude to you, so you will know."

There was respondent emotion and sincerity in the doctor's voice as he gave reply, "In addition to the personal satisfaction and pride I receive from the success of my operations, it is moments like this that are the ultimate reward! I thank you for your forthright honesty! You have made me glad I came."

"Will you stay a while and have tea with me? I am sure my nurse is brewing it even now." As she spoke, Nurse Johnson appeared bearing a tray holding a pot of tea and cups and saucers.

The doctor took in the situation and smiled appreciatively, "You ladies, all your captivating genre, have a way with you that no mere man can fathom or resist. God bless you all! I had not thought to visit long... just to say, `hello'. But the charming nature of your invitation makes it impossible for a gentleman to conscientiously refuse. I will happily stay and have a

spot of tea with you, and enjoy every moment of it."
And then, smiling benignly at Nurse Johnson, and
continuing to address Mignonette, "Perhaps your nurse
would like to join us? I am remembering what a helpful
asset she was during those initial days that were touch-
and-go, so to speak, after your accident. You were
much blessed that she was with you at that time."

Nurse Johnson blushed profusely at the extravagant
praise, and Mignonette responded, "Yes, dear, do sit
with us, and fetch Scotty. I'm sure the good Doctor
would like to see the splendid example of his successful
handiwork." Then added, "I don't like leaving him
unattended very long. You never know what might
happen."

The nurse rose abruptly and left, returning at once
with a fussing infant held lovingly in her arms. "He
dislikes having his sleep interrupted," she explained.
"But he's a good baby."

The doctor gestured with extended arms, and the
nurse gently handed the child to him. The baby's frown
immediately blossomed into a smile as he nestled into
the doctor's arms, and he cooed contentedly... reaching
out with his tiny hand and touching the man's face.

"My goodness!" the man exclaimed, "but you are a
sturdy youngster." And then, turning to address the
boy's mother, "I like a child that adjusts quickly and
compatibly to strange environment. It denotes intrinsic
strength of character." Then observed, "The boy's father
must have been quite an example of the complete man."

"Oh, yes!" the child's mother quickly exclaimed.
"Indeed he was... or that is to say, is! I think, too, Scotty
may believe, in his baby mind, you are his father. I talk
to him often about his father returning to us someday

soon. Perhaps too often! But it is my way of combating my loneliness. I hope I can be forgiven for that. It is such a small thing, and gives me so much comfort."

The doctor smiled patiently. "Talking is good therapy, for the listener as well as the speaker, especially if it is constructive. And also, a mother's generous conversation with her baby, teaches the child at an early age, to think and relate, and to more easily express himself." Then added, with an amenable smile and a twinkle in his eye, "That's why God endowed woman with the penchant for opulent speech." Then summed up his philosophy with the cogent phrase, "There's a wisdom to all things."

Nurse Johnson laughed in appreciation of the doctor's display of diplomacy. "That's the nicest way I've ever heard it said that women talk a lot. You should have been in the diplomatic service."

"I am, in a way," the doctor replied. "A good bedside manner is a form of diplomacy." He gave the tiny child an affectionate squeeze and a peck on his cheek, and handed him to Mignonette. "I think it wise, considering the child's tentatively formed mind-set, that he not be allowed too close an association with the male gender for just now. It may induce a mixing of identities in his mind regarding his future relationship with his father when that gentleman returns, and the resulting confusion lead to a serious problem. An infant's psyche is a sensitive and fragile entity, and remains as yet much of a mystery to medical science. It is better to be safe than sorry, as any wise man will tell you."

The baby complained momentarily, and then snuggled comfortably against his mother's breast . . .a manifestation of the truth the doctor had just expressed

... and was soon sleeping peacefully, blissfully unaware he was the subject of a concerned topic of conversation.

The conversation continued in the same enlightening vein until Mignonette's distinguished guest had finished his second cup of French tea, at which time he arose somewhat reluctantly and announced his professional duties pressed the necessity of his return to the hospital. "I currently have a patient whose condition demands special attention, as most of them do, so I mustn't be away too long. The main reason for my visit was to tell you I will gladly accept the invitation to attend your upcoming social, and to specify the time it will be most convenient for me and my staff to attend. Will two weeks from today fit in with your schedule? There will be approximately ten guests."

"Oh yes," Mignonette replied with enthusiasm. "That will be just fine. I will call the caterer tomorrow, and let him know." She smiled, "Come with your best appetite; I have an extravagant menu planned. And there will be an orchestra to indulge the artistic appetite of those who love music. I may even sing a few of my old cabaret songs... if coaxed," she added, impishly.

"Oh yes! Missy sings beautifully," the nurse interjected. "And such a wonderful voice! She used to be the featured vocalist at the best nightclub in Paris during the years of the war."

"I shall look forward to hearing you sing, Miss Lescaut, and I must say the remarkable beauty of your garden bears tribute to your knowledge and appreciation of the artistic. At this early moment I predict your party will be the outstanding choice as the premier social success of the season! Most certainly it will be mine!" He smiled graciously, and added, "And I thank you now for a most stimulating afternoon and the pleasure of your company." He bowed and took his leave.

After he had gone Nurse Johnson sighed and said, "What a fine gentleman he is... and so wise and successful. He would make most any woman happy." She sighed again, wistfully, and with no attempt at concealment. At that time, sighing was still fashionable with maiden ladies.

"Yes, almost any woman," Mignonette replied, with a smile of commiseration for her friend, but with a tone that repudiated any similarity of personal feeling on her part. The involuntary sigh that accommodated her remark was freighted with nostalgia, and was indigenous to the ever-haunting memory of the past.

The following two weeks were busy ones for Mignonette. Her thoughts, when she was not attending her duties of motherhood, were focused on the planning and preparation of her approaching party. She was indeed resolved in making the occasion the outstanding event of the local social season! She had been optimally inspired by the contagious enthusiasm the good doctor had displayed with his earlier non-medical prognosis of its brilliant success, and she tacitly thanked him for the added motivation and encouragement.

Nurse Johnson was her usual helpful self. When she wasn't minding the baby or doing other chores, she was running errands into town, collecting items that Mignonette needed to enhance and facilitate the festive aspect of the approaching social occasion.

Time passed swiftly, as it will do when busy minds and hands are occupied with the fulfillment of a cherished goal. The season was now deep into the bounty of Alpine spring. The foliage of Mignonette's garden was a riot of sensuous colors. And the fabled apple tree, the guardian of her hopes and the symbol to her future, towered in imposing magnificence, the cynosure of this effusion of lush splendor... and an attestation to the reality and truth of God's promise of eternal life. Its up-flung branches, heavily laden now with the burgeoning manifestation of incipient fruit, seemed raised as if in silent benediction to that same Almighty Creator.

And so at last the much anticipated day came, and all was ready. At the far end of her spacious, high-walled garden, her architectural gardener had originally constructed a moderate but fashionable amphitheater and a small stage for entertainment purposes. To accommodate any anticipated small audience, a number of individual refreshment tables and cushioned chairs were provided in convenient proximity to, and facing the stage, encapsulated under a sheltering pavilion. It was here that she would entertain her guests in regal fashion. All this elaboration had originally been conceived and implemented in preparation for the welcoming ceremony of her lover's eventual return.

The catering crew, consisting of a maitre de, a chef and an entourage of uniformed waitresses arrived about noon, and began preparation of her planned full-course dinner. Nurse Johnson helped where she was needed.

The members of the ten-piece orchestra she had arranged for appeared a little later, and positioned their instruments on the stage acoustically near Mignonette's baby grand piano, and began familiarizing themselves with the musical pieces Mignonette had selected. To facilitate their preparation and also to condition her voice, she vocalized through a few selections with them. Soon satisfied that she was in good voice, she directed her attention to welcoming the guests, who had begun to arrive.

They came almost at once, fifteen in all... nurses and medical staff that could be spared for a short interval away from their patients, and several of their close friends from nearby Lausanne who had heard repute of the celebrated singer from the famous Golden Peacock in Paris.

She was at her vibrant best now. The nostalgic sensation of those halcyon years before the war, rushed unbidden now upon her, suffusing her consciousness with a transport of familiar and nearly forgotten fulfillment! For a precious interval the onus of her haunting sadness and great loss faded into recession under the excitement and stimulation of the present festive circumstances. Only to return at fleeting intervals, when stark reality invaded her doldrums of tranquility to remind her of the tragic episode that had deprived her of the connubial joy she had so completely and wholeheartedly embraced as her own, but had so precipitously lost by the malfeasance of an inimical fate.

The good Doctor Vandermeer's optimistic prognosis for the success of her social extravaganza had been a paradigm of prophesy. At the outset it gave indication of exceeding the attainment that the kindness of his words had implied. Everything had an air of elegance. The food was delicious, and the conversation inspiring. And as the piece de resistance of that most delightful afternoon, Mignonette reprised her role as the nonpareil songstress of the Golden Peacock, transfixing her audience with the vocal beauty and impassioned eloquence of the legendary bird of song, establishing now on the local scene, her famous Parisian sobriquet as the "Golden Nightingale of the City of Lights."

Shimmering gold was the texture of her hair... resonant gold, the texture of her voice... and virgin gold, the texture of the passion in her heart!

And though most were aware that she was an unwed mother, and empathized with her pain, no reference was ever made of it in her presence, for they knew the circumstances that had made it so, and they loved and admired her for her courage and unflagging loyalty to a love that had betrayed her happiness! There is always a tragic abundance of that in the aftermath of any great war. The stark reality of life plays no favorites, and is without remorse.

And so, buoyed on the crest of this upbeat wave of enjoyment and conviviality, the day and its pleasures slipped by all too swiftly, and it came time for the finale... her signature song. There were those among the guests who wondered if she would essay to sing a song which, although traditionally demanded, was so emotionally explosive, and she, herself, questioned for a moment if such were wise. But she would not disappoint her audience: This was their party... and hers! There would be no deference given to sadness on this night! And so she sang their song, the mantra to the lost happiness of her and her lover. There was no room for tears in a heart filled with love, and her voice was resonant with the power of consummate inspiration. And all those listening who knew her story, were transfixed with awe at the dimension of such unflagging courage and loyalty to an ideal... equally as much as they were by the beauty of her voice and its offered benediction.

It had been an evening charged with nobleness, humility and a consummation of new friendships, and reluctantly the happy guests bid their farewells and took their leave, each nurturing the intimate feeling of having been welcomed into the confidence of this gracious hostess, and into the glory and the mystery of the cross she had for so long so singly and nobly borne, so great had been the effect of the penetrating and encompassing poignancy of the song's implication! And many there were who, in leaving the precincts of the sheltering garden, touched the tree in passing and added their own silent prayer to the song's incantation, to enhancei ts charm and fortify its opportunity for success!

Mignonette sat alone now in her deserted garden, relaxing beneath the comforting branches of her apple tree, idly reviewing the activities of the evening, and pleasurably acknowledging the success of the party had exceeded her most optimistic expectations.

Perhaps an hour had passed since the soiree had ended. The orchestra and catering personnel had tidied up and departed, and Nurse Johnson was in the house attending to baby Scotty and her usual domestic chores. The setting sun was nearing the western horizon, and the emerging luminance of a full moon overhead promised to soften the shadows that threatened encroachment into the garden. As the excitement of the eventful evening gradually dissipated, her mind sobered and became more discretionary and her thoughts more nostalgic. She knew the party had really been about her and the mystery of her past... her association and intimate connection with a conspicuous hero of the recent war. In the eyes of each guest, she had seen the obvious expression of sympathy for her prolonged ordeal and the concomitant curiosity that was too awkward to articulate into a question, and which would have been too personal and too sensitive to have been adequately answered.

She had seen the number of departing guests touch the tree as they passed from the garden... had seen their lips move in silent tribute, and she had felt the tears that had risen to her heart in response. Remembering it now, she began to sing, softly at first, to herself, the song of the apple tree. Wildly, desperately hoping all this concerted magic of the evening would summon the power to bring her lost love back to her at last! For a wild, disordered moment she almost believed it would happen. Her voice rose into a crescendo of passion... her appeal calling out through time and space. He would come. His love was as great as hers. He would surely come. He had promised.

Her voice died away into a sob, overwhelmed by the tears that flooded in upon her. She struggled to reclaim reality! Then a sound nearby interrupted her attention, and she turned quickly and arose, to discover the nature of the source. Dimly through the shadows she beheld the indistinct figure of a man... tall, he was, and imposing! Dear, merciful God... was it... could it be... She reeled and grew suddenly faint... and would have fallen, but strong hands caught and held her.

"Miss Lescaut, are you all right? I'm sorry if I startled you." The man's voice was gentle and solicitous.

She recognized who it was then, and struggled to compose herself, as she pushed him gently away. "Oh, it's you, Doctor Vandermeer. Yes, I'm quite all right now, but you gave me quite a shock for a moment. My thoughts were caught in the past, I'm afraid. I certainly didn't expect to see you so soon again."

He winced inwardly at the abruptness of her words, but tacitly forgave the rebuff, realizing it was not intended as such, and that his sudden unexpected intrusion into the realm of her solitude had caused a momentary disruption of her poise. His immediate words of apology gave evidence of regret for his unfortunate impropriety, and then, choosing his words carefully, as though apprehensive of the impression their impact might have, he essayed an explanation for his surprising appearance. "The memory of an unfortunate occurrence in which I was a protagonist, has been plaguing me for longer than I care to admit... an incident that also concerned you to a great degree. I had thought it a good chance to find you alone at this time, for the matter is private to you and me, and I had hoped to keep it that way... for your sake as well as mine. I pray you do not find my presence too intrusive at this rather unseemly hour. I would sadly deplore inconveniencing you, but I have far too long delayed giving the proper attention to this particularly sensitive matter, in consideration of any possible negative repercussion. And I will leave even now, if you wish it. I have no desire to distress you. Indeed, to the contrary, I have every wish and reason to avoid such an imposition. However, I pray you will find the magnanimity within your heart to hear what I must tell you." He paused, allowing her the opportunity to acquiesce to his request, or to refuse it.

The doctor's humility and his eloquent and almost desperate sincerity induced the resurgence of Mignonette's composure, and persuaded her cooperation. "I'm sorry I seemed so abrupt, Doctor," she apologized. "Of course you are always welcome here. You could never intrude. Won't you please tell me what it is that troubles you so? I would like to help, if I am able." Her contrition, in turn, served to reassure him, and he hastened on like a man on a vital crusade, with time a precious premium.

"A long time ago a misadventure occurred involving us," he began, "an insidious incident that never should have happened, but that afforded me the opportunity of doing you a great and vital service... but also gravely compromised my social position and my career. And as a man of unimpeachable honor, I must clear up in your mind any negative misconception you may entertain pertaining to my character and honor! And only the hard truth will accomplish that. I care little for what others may think! What you think of me is vital to my happiness! When you have heard my story you will either condemn or forgive me... but it must be told! I must obtain your belief." And so, with studied determination he addressed his meticulous efforts to relating the onerous detail of the ancient escapade that haunted his peace of mind, and the revelation that would support any challenge to his equilibrium of justice. And so began his intriguing tale:

"My story begins just before the outbreak of the recent war. I had just received my doctor's degree from the University of Berlin, and was immediately conscripted into the German medical corps against my wishes. I hated war... it was so pointless and barbaric ... but it was either that or prison. It was a difficult choice for me to make at first, but I eventually realized I could at least alleviate the suffering of the wounded, many of whom felt as I did about war and the criminal aspect of its nature. And so I accepted an appointment as major in the elite Nazi Medical Corps in charge of a hospital near the forward lines. I was a trauma surgeon, but my specialty was the treatment of head injuries. After France fell to the Nazis my hospital was moved to Paris. I also administered to the wounds of many French prisoners, which procedure was frowned upon by the higher echelon of the military. But I persisted in the practice until it was finally accepted. It was then that I felt completely justified in my choice of military service rather than submitting to imprisonment. One cannot progress in this world without making positive commitments to his loyalties and beliefs."

He paused for a moment, noting with relief and encouragement, the rapt attention his listener was paying to his recital. He resumed his story with renewed optimism. "It was at about this time that I became aware of your existence. One night, seeking relaxation and relief from the appalling rigors of attending the wounds of shattered bodies and empathizing with their suffering, I spent a few hours in a Parisian nightclub enjoying the music and atmosphere away from the horrors of war. It was called the Golden Peacock. From that night on I spent my evenings there, whenever I was off duty." He paused again; this time carefully considering the propriety of what he knew the truth of his story must reveal.

"Some people believe they ascend to Heaven after they depart from this world. I found mine here on Earth... such was the contrast to me between the raging Hell of war and what I had finally discovered in the precincts of a Parisian nightclub. If Hell is indigenous to Earth, why not Heaven, also?"

He paused again, gathering the necessary courage for his next words... his eyes, that feasted their hunger across her beautiful face were filled with an adoration that even the twilight was hard beset to conceal. "There was a girl... a woman, possessing of a matchless beauty I had never seen before, nor conceived of... even in my wildest dreaming. She was the vocalist there... and her voice was gifted with the music of angels!"

With a great shock Mignonette suddenly realized at last... it was she of whom he was speaking. In her anguish she cried out, "Don't... Oh please don't! You mustn't. You know my heart belongs to another. What you are saying can only demean you... and bring me great distress."

"No," he said, shaking his head vehemently, "You mistake me! I am not making love to you. I would never do that! To do so would be sacrilegious! The love you hold for another, and your devotion to it, I cherish! Its nobleness, I hold sacrosanct... inviolate . . .as I do my own. I only tell you of my love for you because you are deserving of that knowledge! I believed it would make you proud to realize you have inspired so great a love in the steadfast hearts of two. There are some who preach there is no pride in Heaven. This I do not believe... for it is natural to have pride in an act well taken... to receive comfort from the knowledge of a noble attribute intrinsically possessed! There are many angels, and a few still walk among us on this Earth!"

There were tears in his eyes that she could hardly see in the gathering dusk, but she knew they were there, for she detected them in the passion of his voice. "Some people," he continued, "live their lives without love. May God pity them. And some there are whose lives embrace a great love that endures unrequited! God does not pity them, for in His annals they are of the Elite . . .for God IS love. I impugn you: do not pity me... for I have a certain happiness you will never know. And I envy no one... because of it. I am sorry that my clumsiness misled you. Do not be embarrassed. The fault was mine. Your reaction was proper and well taken under the circumstances, and only adds to my admiration for you. You are of a rare class." He paused once more before continuing with his story that was only half told. "There is another reason why I thought it important to reveal my feelings for you: You will discover later in my story that it will explain and ameliorate, if not entirely justify, the harshness of the extreme action I found necessary to take."

Except for her one protest, Mignonette had remained silent for the entire length of the doctor's story. Rousing now, and remembering her role as hostess, she remarked, "Your narrative is very inspirational, and I must hear more of it, but I seem to have forgotten my good manners. I'll have my maid brew us some tea, and we'll sit over there at one of those party tables near the stage while you finish your story."

And so, sipping their tea and more comfortably at ease, the doctor began the final segment of his tale, while Mignonette listened raptly as he recounted the details of their memorable encounter with the SS officer who had attacked her, and his own vital involvement in the episode.

"Much of what I am about to say will be completely revelatory to you because of the necessary secrecy with which it was handled afterwards, and your impaired mental and emotional condition at the time it occurred, therefore you may understandably find it hard to believe; but every word I tell you will be the unembellished truth! I am the only one who knows what really happened that fateful night! I was there . . .thank God I was there... and it was I who orchestrated the final and inevitable solution necessitated by the patent atrocity of the conditions involved, and the contingent threat of any possible repercussion to the innocent participants!"

The vivid picture of that night stormed virulently back into his memory as he warmed to his task, and he arose and began pacing in suppressed agitation as he struggled for equilibrium to continue the searing revelation of his emotional tale. "Forgive me! This is more difficult than I had thought! Perhaps sharing its burden with you will diminish its onus a little," he added, hopefully.

"It started several weeks after I had adopted the custom of spending my all too infrequent leisure evenings escaping the rigors of attending the hapless wounded, and enjoying the more peaceful atmosphere of the Golden Peacock. Listening to the music of your voice was a welcome anodyne to the abrasive stress that daily confronted me, and to the assault of its deteriorating effect upon my peace-loving nature. It was a Sunday; I remember it well! Before entering the sanctuary of the Golden Peacock that night, and enjoying the relief of temporary oblivion to the madness of war it offered me, I had spent some reflective time in a neighboring church praying for the early end to hostilities.

"The song you were singing that memorable night as I entered was an old British favorite from the First War: 'It's a Long Way to Tipperary.' Do you remember? Your selections were limited to songs of French and British origin in those days, for the United States had not yet entered the war."

"Yes, I remember," Mignonette almost whispered. "It happened a long time ago... more than five years." She shuddered as his words brought back the unacceptable memory of the past! "But its haunting memory still disturbs my peace of mind! Would to dear God I could forget!"

The good doctor smiled wryly in commiseration. "To forget, you must first remember! It is the mystery of it that plagues you ... the dark, empty places into which your desperate imagination probes in its effort to remember something you never knew... hoping to uncover a clue that will tell you the thing you fear most did not happen! We will examine the details together, and when you have learned the whole truth, your subconscious will release the undeserved onus of guilt you feel... and you will be free! Always, the solution to a problem lies in knowing the truth of it. Trust me. I have a doctorate in the knowledge and treatment of the known anomalies of the brain as they pertain both to the psychological and to the surgical. In addition, my own creative experience has advanced the scientific understanding of its function, and has provided me with the optimal solution." He paused to observe her reaction to his extravagant claim of superior knowledge and, noting the expression of credence and trust within the depth of her beautiful eyes, he picked up the thread of his story once more, continuing with an air of reassurance.

"Your audience was comprised of a large number of the German military personal, and I marveled at your patent disregard for the hostility your vocal selection would receive, and the courage and patriotism you displayed in flaunting it! But I winced at the danger you invited! There were a few who responded with sporadic disapproval, but many of the military applauded enthusiastically, for your beauty of voice and appearance were too dominant to be ignored. You persisted, undaunted! They, too, were impressed by your personal disregard for nationalistic criticism.

"When your song had ended you curtsied charmingly and gave a terse and appealing explanation: `I sing for the muse of art... and for the sake of your entertainment. I thank you most gratefully for your approval!' Do you remember?" He smiled encouragingly, inviting her recollection.

"Yes, I do recall the incident, now that you mention it. Your memory is remarkable."

"Not so remarkable," he said, smiling again, apologetically, "When I remind you... forgive me... that I was in love with you."

Mignonette reached out suddenly in emotional response, and pressed his hand for a moment. "My dear friend!" She felt a certain rapport for this man... for his sensitivity and his deeper distress because of it. He had suffered his burden of unrequited love far longer than she had endured hers. Then, startled by the unanticipated emotion of his response to her innocent gesture of empathy, she quickly withdrew her hand, for she felt the trembling of his. Yes, there was no doubt remaining in her mind... The man had surely loved her... deeply and long.

He continued implacably with his story, ignoring the emotional interruption as though it had not occurred. "There was this small group of officers, all members of the elite Schutzstaffel, Hitler's S.S. Guard, sitting at a table next to mine, who were hostilely reactive to your nonchalant display of patriotism. One especially, was known as a troublemaker who, it was rumored, was ruthless in his treatment of women, and openly boasted of it. I made special note to keep an eye on him. He knew me well, for we had, on one occasion, been embroiled in a physical altercation in which I had come out victorious. And he had been reprimanded severely for his part in it, as at that time I was held in some favor by those in the higher echelon of the military. As a matter of fact, I was promoted to colonel... although I was already in line for it due to the sterling performance of my hospital staff and the successful treatment of our patients.

"Most of the German military had left to return to quarters by the time you had sung your finale. Only this S.S. officer still remained. I sat, vigilantly alert, as you made your way past the customers, and out through the front entrance. This S.S. officer, his name was Schmidt, suspiciously arose and disappeared out through the entrance a few yards behind you. Realizing you were very possibly in imminent danger, I, too, immediately exited the same door and stepped out into the blackness of the night. I could barely see him some yards ahead of me, and you had disappeared completely into the night, for the City of Lights had become a tomb of darkness at that late hour, brought on by the war. But good fortune was with us that fateful night, thank God, for I knew where you lived, as I had earlier adopted the role of invisible chaperon to you on several occasions and had the advantage of knowing your probable destination.

"It was difficult to keep my quarry in sight and still remain unobserved, so I also soon lost sight of him! I realized later, you must have become apprehensive you were being followed, and had increased your pace; and that he, in turn, had increased his. In desperation I hurried on, traversing the narrow, twisting streets that are so indigenous to Paris... hoping to arrive in time to be of any needed assistance to you.

"When I came to your room, with the tiny light

above your door shining dimly through the darkness, my heart sank in dismay. No one was in sight. Had I come too late. In my helpless position I was near panic! Had he overtaken you en route in the darkness? Dear God . . .I prayed it was not so. And then I heard a muffled scream. It came from within your room. My prayers had been partially answered. There was still time.

"With a surge of energy and a terrible purpose, I flung my weight against the intervening barrier. It shattered into pieces under the fervor of my wrath, and I stood within the room, an angel of vengeance.

"The sight that met my scourging gaze still brings a shudder even now as I speak of it. You were struggling weakly... futilely, locked in this monster's profane grasp... while his predatory hands were tearing at your garments. You were plainly in a helpless and fainting mode. Someone would surely die that night." Her narrator paused, fighting to retain his equanimity of emotion.

"Your assailant turned in shocked surprise, to face this sudden and unexpected threat, an expression of mingled hatred and terror on his face. There was the haunted fear of death in his eyes, but the intent of death to his adversary was there, too.

"I leaped toward him, and he released you from his grasp in order to defend himself against my onslaught, allowing you to fall inertly to the floor. As I reached him he swung a vicious blow at my head with his fist, which I deftly avoided. Then, with all the impetus of the accumulated rage that had been building within me, I struck back at him, catching him in the throat with the edge of my open hand. He went down like a poleaxed ox. He was dead in a moment. I was aware I had killed him, but I felt no regret. I was only grateful that I had arrived in time to rescue you from a terrible fate.

"I hastened to where you lay, picked you up and placed you gently upon your bed. You opened your eyes for a horrified instant... flashing me a glance of great alarm and shock, and lapsed back into a traumatic coma! Things were happening so fast, and I was so agitated at that time, I did not realize until much later that you must have thought I was your attacker renewing his assault upon you.

"From what I had witnessed, and by your appearance to my trained physician's eye, I knew you had not been physically harmed, so I drew a blanket over you to keep you warm, hoisted the dead officer across my shoulder, and quickly stepped out into the shielding darkness and obscurity, just as your landlord, aroused by all the disturbing commotion, approached the open doorway to your room. His opportune appearance set my mind at rest as to your immediate safety.

"I thought it wise to dispose of my victim's body, thereby allowing the entire incident to remain shrouded in unresolvable mystery, so I set out urgently for the river. My foremost consideration was to shield you from any threat of recrimination. Being intimately conversant with the mind-set of the Nazi military, I knew they would hold you to blame. Even with me as your witness it would have been touch-and-go.

Another consideration disturbed me: You had obviously seen my face as you revived momentarily from your unconscious state. Would its image remain in your conscious mind, or would it lie sequestered and festering in your subconscious psyche? I could not be certain which condition persisted. So, as a precautionary measure, I never set foot in the Golden

Peacock again! I feared you might inadvertently recognize me, and our dangerous secret would be exposed. The repercussions would have been disastrous, for both of us! And when I had you brought to my hospital after your riding accident, I observed the same precautions... never permitting you a glimpse of my face. This I did, for a much different reason: I feared the possible disastrous impact such a traumatic revelation might have on your critically unstable condition.

"Well, that's the crux of the story. Schmidt's disappearance was spoken of intermittently, for a short while; and then no more was said. I heard later, he had been classified as a deserter. In either case, it was a fitting end for one such as he."

As he finished his verbal replication of the details that occurred that fateful night, he watched her face closely to ascertain her emotional reaction, hoping to find an expression of relief there. He was not disappointed... but commingled with her feeling of relief and emancipation from shame was the more dominant expression of admiration and measureless gratitude for the man who, at the risk of his own life and reputation, and without selfish motive or any thought of mercenary reward, had successfully managed such a hazardous feat... and never spoke of it to anyone. She knew then, if there had been any doubt before, that he truly loved her.

There were tears in her eyes, and tears in her voice as she spoke her heart to him: "Oh, my gallant friend... my truly gallant and most remarkable friend. You have secured that most pristine position in my heart forever. If I should ever love again, it would surely be you." Her restraint broke under the stress of her confused but sincere emotions, and she was weeping uncontrollably now, in a spate of joy and regret! But, alas... she could not savor a love she could not feel... and Doctor Vandermeer knew that unrequited love must always walk alone.

The doctor arose, a light of fulfilled compensation shining across his face. "Dry your precious tears, my much beloved one. I know some of them were for me; but waste them not on such as that. What you have shown me tonight is more than I could ever have expected, and will amply suffice to warm away the chill of future days, and from which I will draw some happiness forever! I hope what you have learned tonight will serve to erase the guilt you felt, and shine a light into those dark, empty places in your memory. Believe me when I tell you I shall search, and I shall find your errant love for you. Thank you for a wonderful evening." He bowed, still gallant in heart and demeanor, and turned to go. Impulsively she caught him in a grateful embrace for a moment, "Go with God," she said. He smiled, and walked away into the night.

REVELATION

(Part Two)

When Scott Kilmeade awoke in the recovery room many hours after his operation, his first thought was, "Where the hell am I!" And those were his first words, as he articulated them aloud... to no one in particular, and to anyone in general. He heard a door close. "Nurse!" he called. His voice sounded feeble to him. There was no answer. "Nurse!" He tried to shout. Still no response. And why was it so dark, he wondered. He tried to lift his arms, but could not. He became worried! There was something here he did not understand!

He knew he must be in a hospital... in bed. He could feel the softness of a mattress beneath him, and the smell of antiseptics inundated the room. His concern grew into alarm... and his awareness of a modicum of reality increased with it. His head was throbbing with excruciating pain from his exertions. And then a sensation of full awareness smote him... the war. He had been wounded! That damned exploding shell so close to him... and then oblivion!

His aching head was filled with the cacophonous sound of exploding thunder as he tried desperately to sort out the events that had brought him here... wherever 'here' might be; and what were the circumstances that now confronted him?

He heard the door open and close again, and sensed a presence in the room with him. He tried to turn his head in that direction, but could not. "Is someone there?" A tone of impatience had crept into his voice.

"Yes, Colonel Kilmeade. It's Doctor Vandermeer. And I came to tell you everything went just as expected. After nature has been allowed to take its healing course, we will know if the operation has been a complete success. But the procedure itself went smoothly, and I am most optimistic of a favorable prognosis." He paused, eyeing his patient critically. "You may be experiencing some pain right now, in the cranial region, but that is natural, considering the severity of your injury, and the stress from the operation. That will diminish rapidly over time. It appears, from my experienced observation of similar cases, that your condition was not as critically virulent as I had originally anticipated. I think we are justified in expecting the best." Kilmeade's heavily bandaged eyes denied him the reassurance that the smile of optimism on the doctor's face conveyed.

"Tell me, Doctor," Kilmeade said, "Is my head wound the only damage I have suffered?" He waited in dread for the answer to the question he had hesitated to ask, and now subconsciously sought to delay by interpolating an explanation. "I don't seem to be able to move my arms or legs, although I can feel them." His words rushed on, fearfully, "I've still got them, haven't I? Or is that just the phantom sensation you hear about from amputees?" And then he became expectantly silent!

The question was a strange one, under the circumstances, and the doctor was momentarily puzzled by its irrelevance, then quickly dismissed its importance: Patients often spoke irrationally after having been under deep sedation for a long period of time. His quiet laugh was respectful to the occasion, and his subsequent words embraced his patient with consummate relief. "No, Colonel," he replied, "I am happy to tell you that you still have all your God-given appendages. You have been fastened down; a procedure we follow with brain patients as a precaution against any involuntary movement they might make that would cause them harm. I will have the nurse remove your restraints, now that you are conscious and rational. Any questions you may have, I will be glad to answer, at any time. You have nothing to worry about. I have every reason to believe your operation was a complete success. We will know for certain in a few days. In the meantime, you must get all the rest you can. That is the most important consideration right now." He stepped to the door, and just before he disappeared he turned and said, "I will send the nurse in to attend to your restraints. She will remain at bedside to respond to your wishes, and I will be on call if needed. Again, rest well, and I will check on you first thing tomorrow. Goodnight." He motioned to the nurse, and she followed him out of the room.

"I want to caution you: Answer no specific questions he may ask you, as to the present date. There may be a discrepancy in his memory regarding his relationship to time. I will find out for sure tomorrow when I question him more closely. A shock to him now could prove harmful. He must be allowed to adjust slowly to proper time orientation. I'll see you in the morning... Goodnight."

Immediately after the doctor left, Kilmeade's mind began to explore the precincts of his newly established past... probing into the limit of its familiar depths, unaware that the succeeding five years that had elapsed since his casualty at the battle of Meaux, and which the devious antics of his memory had earlier reclaimed, was now lost to him again! He was back again on square one. But his consciousness rested on solid ground at last, and his mind would adjust normally now, after the effects of the congestion and swelling created from the operation had dissipated. The shock of an operation of such critical magnitude performed on the brain, has by itself a traumatic impact on the patient. Doctor Vandermeer was the only surgeon, at that time, able and fully qualified to conduct an operation of such a delicate nature. The man was truly a surgical genius!

The next morning, after his patient had been given his daily bath and a fresh dressing gown and bedding, and had finished his carefully selected breakfast, Dr. Vandermeer looked in on him, as he had promised. "Good morning, Colonel. How do you feel today? I trust you slept well."

"Good morning, Doctor," Kilmeade replied, smiling cheerfully. "Yes, I feel much better today. My headache's about gone, and," he added, smiling somewhat sheepishly, "I am fully aware now, I still have my arms and legs. I apologize for asking that silly question about them last night. Under the circumstances I hope you will understand and forgive me."

The doctor returned his smile, "Don't give it another thought, Colonel. If I told you some of the questions I am asked by my patients, after their operations, you wouldn't believe it. I may write a book about it someday... without mentioning any names, of course." He laughed indulgently.

Then adopting a more professional attitude, he continued in a serious tone: "I am going to ask you a question or two with the purpose in mind of ascertaining the stability of your mental state. First, give me your name and military rank."

Kilmeade promptly replied, "My name is Scott Kilmeade, major in the United States Army." He smiled, "That was easy."

The doctor nodded, "Fine. Now tell me, as near as you can, the approximate date, as of today." It was a critical question!

Kilmeade thought carefully for a moment or two before he answered, weighing the circumstances and calculating as closely as he could. "I can't be sure, of course, but I would venture to say it is close to the first week in March of 1945. How's that?"

"Excellent, Major. That's close enough. That's all the questions I have at this time. I will have more as your condition progresses. What is vital to you right now is acquiring as much rest and peace of mind as possible. Your brain needs all the rest you can give it. Keep your thinking down to a necessary minimum. It will hasten your complete recovery. I will leave now, and let you sleep." He turned to go, but was halted by a response from his patient.

"I have an important question that I must know the answer to, before I can have any peace of mind. And then I will follow your recommendations to the letter, Doctor. I must know how the fortunes of the war are going for the Allies... the outcome of the battle at Meaux! Tell me what I must hear, and I will rest!"

The doctor gave him a beaming smile, "It goes well, my heroic soldier! The battle is won... and there will be peace... for all of us! Rest now, and we will talk again." He quietly withdrew from his patient's bedside, feeling assured of Kilmeade's optimal recovery.

Just outside, in the hallway, he met the day nurse returning, and imposed the following warning, "Your patient believes he is yet a major in rank. Be sure to use that designation when addressing him, as he is temporarily locked within the time slot when the battle of Meaux was fought. It is absolutely vital, for the present, that his belief continue as it is, without the possible shock of premature adjustment. He must not be allowed contact with anyone or anything that might interfere with his present mind-set! Answer no questions he may ask in that area. Refer him to me. We must encourage him to avoid the process of thinking, as much as possible. His mind must rest! I repeat: His mind must rest... It is vital!" It was the same charge of responsibility he had imposed on the other two nurses who attended Kilmeade, as well as all the other staff members at the hospital. Beyond any doubt Kilmeade was under the most advanced scientific care at that time available to the practice of medicine, and orchestrated by the most success-oriented brain specialist then existent.

Doctor Richards had left the hospital and taken up temporary lodging at their hotel in town to avoid inadvertent contact with his friend. The time slot that Kilmeade's mind was now locked in precluded him of any knowledge of their acquaintance, and seeing him at that time could cause harmful repercussions.

Several days went by, and Kilmeade was allowed to sit up for short periods of time, well supported by pillows strategically placed around him. But he was restricted from indulging in any unnecessary conversation. His mind occasionally strayed to thoughts concerning his beloved Mignonette but, scrupulously heeding his doctor's advice and warning, he would quickly dismiss them from his mind. He was staunchly dedicated to obtain optimal recovery from his wound as soon as possible to enable him to more quickly attend his personal affairs. Most of his hours were spent in restful sleep.

Always following the doctor's prescribed regimen, his activity was gradually increased until, by the beginning of the third week, he was permitted the freedom of the hospital garden, with a nurse in close attendance. Walking in the sunlight and enjoying the fresh air hastened his convalescence. Sometime during that period the bandages had been removed from his eyes, and normal sight had returned. Gradually his eyes were allowed to accustom themselves to the light so long denied them, sheltered at first behind dark glasses. Kilmeade accepted this change of condition without comment, as the doctor had not spoken to him of his blindness after the operation, for obvious reasons. And at that interval of time he was unaware he had been blind.

Each day his physical stability improved, until by the end of the month his natural health had been restored to him. Only his mind yet remained as it was, locked in the time slot of the past. He grew restless. He had been patient long enough! His memory told him it had been more than a month since that fateful time, the night before the deadly battle at Meaux, and he fretted that he had not heard from Mignonette. Why had she not come to visit him in the hospital during his protracted convalescence. The more he thought about it, the more disquieted he became. And then, there were those strange, nagging dreams he had been having lately: A kindly man, a complete stranger to him, who pervaded his slumbers, and was there with him when he fought that melodramatic duel with some ungodly ruffian. That was when he started having those severe headaches, and it made him wonder if his operation has been a failure. All this contrived to make him disagreeable, and more and more he sought the solitude of his own company. The hospital garden was his favorite spot, and he refused the company of a nurse now, when he was there.

On this day, as he sat alone in his favorite lounge chair, enjoying the summer sunshine and fresh mountain air, a drowsiness seized him, and his mind began drifting into the welcome serenity of peaceful slumber, for the ache in his head was throbbing again. Suddenly a familiar sound, sweet and haunting, came to him from out of the distance past... the empty space of time far greater than he knew! Visual flashes of the forgotten long ago besieged his thoughts. His once handicapped mind was now stirring into life from the catalyst of a love too towering to die... too noble, too vital to longer remain in dire sufferance imprisoned within a memory to which he was not privy. Its impetus... the magnitude of its significance, shocked him back into reality. Wide awake now, he wondered for a moment if the phenomenon were the precipitation from a dream. But there it was again... as faint as a whisper, but as clear to him as the clarion call of a military bugle to his audio-clairvoyant ear... indelibly distinguishable on the morning air! It was no dream. It was his true-love calling to him! And all at once he was whole again! He remembered all of everything. Some mysterious and inexplicable transformation was taking place inside his astonished head! All the memories that had ever belonged to him flooded in upon him now. He was a man twice blessed: The magic scalpel of a genius had restored his sight, and Love once more was offering back his life to him. His throbbing headache was gone... and would never return.

Possessed with an ecstatic joy too overpowering to brook any restraint, and driven by the impugning thought that each passing moment of delay before he and his love were in each other's arms was a sacrilege, he leaped to his feet and was off in the direction from whence the sound had come. He knew the source was close by... perhaps a mile or two; certainly within walking distance, and he hastened onward to ameliorate his aching heart, and keep his promised rendezvous with Mignonette and destiny.

He maintained his eager pace for some twenty minutes, pausing reluctantly every now and then to catch his breath, for the terrain was uneven, and he had not yet completely regained the advantage of his full physical strength. His efforts brought him at length up behind a beautiful walled garden, with a lovely white cottage just beyond that fronted on the main roadway. He made his way around to the garden gate and peered into the enclosed interior, from where the source of the elusive melody he pursued seemed to be. Seeing no one yet, he opened the heavy iron gate and stepped inside. He took a few tentative steps deeper into the garden, reluctant to disturb the faithful singer his heart had loved all those many years, and undesirous of interrupting the intoxicating enchantment of the song that had been the integral component of the chain that would facilitate their reunion and secure reclamation of their love.

Almost timidly his eyes searched for the object of his quest, as he fortified himself against the anticipated emotional impact realization would thrust upon him. Fearfully his eyes came to rest on the recumbent figure of a young woman in a cushioned chair beside a table, with her back to him. Her golden hair that he remembered so well, lay in tumbled curls about the alabaster beauty of her shoulders. And as he stared in speechless wonder and fulfillment, he heard her voice rise into a crescendo of unrequited passion and break off into a sob. And then he heard another voice, that of a child, soft and comforting, "Don't cry, Mommy, he will come. I know he will." Tiny arms appeared, flung around the woman's neck... holding tight among her curls. A small boy's face came into view, nestling lovingly beside hers in a tender gesture of love and commiseration. It was a sight the spellbound watcher would indelibly remember the remainder of his life! And this was the new beginning of that life.

Sometimes, in the life of a special few, after interminable suffering from the ravages of a great travail has run the cruelty of its course, there is an interval of disbelief, when reality becomes a fantasy and credence becomes the incredible! For a moment his mind fought for rationality... lost in a delirium of joy.

The sight was more than Kilmeade could bear in silence. In a pent up flood of words he cried out with an anguished voice, "Mignonette! Oh, my beloved Mignonette! I have come at last... as you can see. I am here. I have kept my sacred vow... Just as you have so faithfully kept yours." He rushed to her in a few swift strides, flung his arms about her and crushed her to his breast in a fervent embrace.

At the sound of Kilmeade's voice Mignonette had arisen in shocked astonishment and turned in disbelief to confront the incredible, as the boy released his hold and slipped to the floor... stepping back in wonder. He was the first to give answer. "Oh, Mommy! Mommy! It's Daddy, isn't it? He has come, just like you said he would." The boy was ecstatic with joy. His child's naiveté persuaded an easily acceptable interpretation of the situation, for a child's reality dwells comfortably in the mythical realm of fairyland, where everything that is beautiful to the heart is true! Often in later years, when speaking of his father or mother, he would lovingly refer to them as the Prince and the Princess.

His mother was unable to make answer for long moments, so overcome was she with emotion... and so tight were Kilmeade's arms about her. The two lovers, locked together in fervent embrace, rocked from side to side, murmuring extravagant words of worship and endearment... savoring the ecstasy that was augmented by the so long protracted dissolution of fulfillment... for an interval of time, lost in subconscious reaction, seeking to recover in a moment all those precious, yet uncapturable empty years that had never existed for them... Years that would have embraced and fostered the essence of their love!

But the small boy, eager to be included in such a momentous emotional resurrection, tugged importunately at his mother's sleeve. "Mommy!" More tugging, "Mommy... Tell Daddy I'm here too." He had inherited the optimistic, the bold and positive characteristics of his illustrious father. He was not to be rebuffed, nor his desires put aside by the focused attention of these two on each other. In his mother's effort over the passing years to gain comfort from her loneliness by commiseration with her son, his naive and honest little mind had been indoctrinated to believe he was an integral factor in this close-knit relationship, and he would now have them share their happiness with his!

His mother, suddenly becoming aware again of her son's presence, disengaged herself from Kilmeade's embrace, and caught her precious child up in her arms.

"I'm so sorry, my darling. Forgive me . . . .us." She handed him to his father. "This bundle of love belongs to you . . . .to us. You left him with me... that terrible morning you went away without saying goodbye. He has been the strength of my hope all these years. I think he knows you as well as I do. You will always be his greatest hero... as you are mine." She paused, and smiled, "His name, of course, is Scott. Those who love him call him Scotty... like I call his wonderful father!"

Kilmeade listened to Mignonette's words of mingled praise and endearment, as he lovingly fondled his son. The boy clung close to his father in wordless happiness! His world was complete, at last. These three were sharing the same emotion.

They sat for a little while, under the apple tree conversing about the years between. "The wound I received at Meaux took my memory and sight away. I've been blind all these years. For a long time no one knew who I was. Bits and pieces of my memory would come and go... but I remembered you eventually. It's all a long story I will fill you in on later. Right now, I must get back to the hospital. When I heard you singing, I'm afraid I left without letting anyone know."

"I'll go with you. My chauffeur will drive us there. I'm not going to let you out of my sight, if I can help it. I received a note from the doctor yesterday, that said he wanted to see me. It was about a work of art he was going to unveil, and he wanted me to be there. He said he would await my convenience."

"This is about as convenient as it gets," Kilmeade answered. "Shall we go, then?"

The little entourage arrived at the hospital in due time. Entering the reception room, they notified the receptionist they were calling in answer to Doctor

Vandermeer's earlier invitation... something about an unveiling of some art object. The woman called the doctor, and he appeared almost at once, perceptibly relieved to see Kilmeade, but showed no surprise by the presence of Mignonette and little Scotty.

"Well," he said, "events are moving rather rapidly, it seems." But he accepted the situation calmly, as was his nature. "I was beginning to think you had gotten lost. But I see you have found yourself, at last!" He smiled at the clever twist of his meaning. Kilmeade smiled too. The man's wit did not escape him.

Mignonette ignored the repartee. "I came along in response to your invitation I received yesterday, to witness the unveiling of some mysterious objet d'art. I did not know you were a connoisseur in that medium. You surprise me."

The doctor smiled. "You will understand, when I tell you I consider my skill as a reconstructive surgeon to be man's highest form of creative art. It is a gift from God, the original creative artist. And this particular example of which we speak, is my most successful creation... the one of which I am the proudest. And although your abortive discovery has denied me some of the drama I had anticipated for this unveiling ceremony, I wish to announce that this paragon of reconstructive art stands unveiled by your side! With the help of God, and for your appreciation, I give you the product of modern medicine, the `whole man'... Colonel Scott Kilmeade!" He bowed toward Kilmeade, extending his arm in a formal gesture of presentation.

Mignonette was near tears. "My dear Doctor Vandermeer, your unveiling rites have suffered no lack of drama! I tremble to visualize my reaction at this moment, had I not experienced the initial traumatic impact of our reunion beforehand!"

"Yes," interjected Kilmeade, "It was better this way, I assure you. I could never share such an intimate scene with anyone else."

The doctor nodded, "You're right, of course. Forgive me if I seemed to have indicated otherwise. Perhaps I have been too intimately involved with both of you to be properly objective. The two of you will always have my blessing... and that includes little Scotty, too! As a matter of fact, because this patient commanded my emotional concern to an unusual degree, I watched him as he walked out of the garden this morning. I knew where he was going; and I let him go... for that same reason you just gave, my dear."

Thinking it best to be completely candid on the subject, and that this was the proper time for it, he continued: "Perhaps I should explain the reason why I harbor such sentiment, if your Mignonette has not already told you. I have known you both during your most recent times of great stress, and have been personally involved each time. What you probably don't know yet, Colonel, is that Mignonette suffered a life-threatening accident five years ago, and she spent several weeks in this hospital under my care. It was 'touch and go' for several days. She was carrying little Scotty at the time, and I delivered him Caesarian section to save the lives of both of them. That was the second occasion where I had the opportunity to render my services. I will let her tell you the details regarding the first time. Suffice it to say, I was near enough at hand to prevent her from being raped or killed by an S.S. officer. In fact, I was forced to kill him."

He paused for a moment, as Kilmeade listened in rapt attention, pondering the doctor's incredible revelation. "This first incident happened several years before you Americans entered the war. I was a colonel, myself, in the German army at that time. I was the senior medical officer, and had jurisdiction over the major traumatic hospital in the forward area of combat." He paused again before concluding his story. "That's about it. So you can easily see why I have difficulty being objective where you two are concerned. I only wished to vicariously share your great happiness on the occasion of your monumental denouement. That is why I had arranged for the unveiling here. But as you walked from the garden this morning, I realized your reunion would be sacred to you, and should be held inviolate of any witness, and so, with a conceivable bit of envy, and a tinge of self-sacrifice, I smiled and was nobly reconciled to mentally visualizing your happiness. The hour of triumph and joy belonged singly to you! I could not interfere! Just knowing of your happiness, and sharing it thus, would be enough!" He fell silent, having expressed what he thought had to be said to lighten the solemnity or tenseness of the moment.

Kilmeade added to the rescue of the situation: "Aren't we all forgetting there is yet another and most important ceremony that must be addressed, and which all our friends are invited to attend. I speak of a belated wedding, military style, that fate denied two trusting lovers long ago."

And so the gala affair was held in due time, midst the surrounding beauty of the hospital garden. Kilmeade, dashingly handsome in his full dress uniform as he stood beside his blushing bride, and Mignonette, resplendent with maidenly beauty, were the perfect picture of marital bliss! Doctor Vandermeer, in a giving mood, gave the bride away; while his great and loyal friend, Doctor Richards stood as best man!

There were several noteworthy and happy reverberations, chief among which was the personal message received from the United States Army Chief of Staff, and expressed in behalf of all the grateful military personnel, living and dead, who had fought so valiantly for concerted victory in the late war, and congratulating him on his marriage and wishing him a long and happy life! In an envelope accompanying the message were a pair of bright silver stars... the insignia of a brigadier general, which were pinned on his uniform at the wedding ceremony by the United States Ambassador to France!

CHAPTER TWELVE
Noblesse Oblige

Those who aspire to the Kingdom of God, and believe in the ultimate salvation of mankind, climb the heights looking ever upward... for heaven is their goal. Every kindness bestowed is a crevice, a fingerhold; each noble deed a ledge, a resting place to renew the strength to sustain the arduous but rewarding ordeal of achieving the crest and ultimate virtue! His vision is ever focused above and ahead, to the trail he must follow, and he sees his way clear in his circumspect advance to his moral objective!

But those who have cast their lot with the Evil One, descend to the Gates of Hell! Their destination downward is a perilous one, for the footing is less secure, albeit travel is more swift. But who has ever heard of any man of true wisdom in a hurry to knowingly court spiritual obliteration!

The Devil's reckoning for service rendered is meted out... and paid in full after the perpetration of each deed. God's spiritual reward comes at the end of the rainbow.

And so this story might have ended here, on an upbeat note, as in one of little Scotty's fairy tales, where the principal characters lived happily ever after. But true life is seldom so simple and kind; and there is no fairyland except that which dwells in the mind of a fool, or the heart of an innocent child. Out from the pages of the unforgiving past, came a relentless reality with its legacy of danger and doom, thrusting its inimical presence into the momentarily peaceful and sedate life of Doctor Hans Vandermeer... and ultimately into that of Scott Kilmeade.

A few days after the wedding, the happy bride and groom, with little Scotty in tow, were back in Marseille preparing their yacht for an extensive honeymoon cruise in the South Pacific, when Kilmeade received an urgent message on the ship's radio. It was from Doctor Richards, who was now working at the hospital, stating that Doctor Vandermeer was in serious peril, and to return at once.

Leaving Mignonette to continue the preparation for their voyage, Kilmeade immediately chartered a private plane, and in less than an hour he was in Lausanne, where he was met by a deeply agitated Doctor Richards. At Richard's suggestion, he secured lodging in a convenient hotel in town where their problem could be discussed in private. And from the story his friend related with distressed emotion, he could easily understand the man's concern.

"This man showed up this morning and deliberately provoked Doctor Vandermeer into a duel. From what I could gather, it had something to do with the death of a brother of his, for which he held the Doctor responsible." And then, apologetically, "I'm terribly sorry to involve you in this mess and disrupt your plans, General, but I know you could never have quite forgiven me if I had not at least sought your advice in the matter. And I would surely have regretted it all my life if I had done less! The good doctor would surely have been killed." He paused, reluctant to reveal his own inadequacy in dealing with violence. "I did not know what else to do. You are the only man I know who would have the definitive solution." He wagged his head in despair, like one transfixed on the horns of a dilemma!

Into the unflagging mind of General Scott Kilmeade, the perennial hero, came the nostalgic but persecuting sound of rolling drums. *Dear and merciful God, when will it end?* his mind cried out in silence! Not again. If ever a man earned his peace, it is I. But his revulsion did not stem the sweep of memory that engulfed him! His rage was momentarily boundless... and he cursed the remorseless fate, ever poised and threatening, that once more offered destruction to his imminent happiness!

There was the thunder of heavy artillery fire again ... echoing in his brain... the rumble and whine of advancing enemy tanks! Overhead the sky was crowded with aircraft! And then they met... the two mightiest machines of war ever mustered. An enemy shell struck near him, throwing him to the torn and bloody earth... and he lay there awaiting the stygian darkness of death. Instead, the shock brought him back to the reality of the present. And like before, his thoughts were of Mignonette. And like before, he knew what he had to do. Again there was only one choice that could be made by an honorable man, a risk he had to take, for only he could do it... and it had to be done! Forgive me, my precious Mignonette. Words spoken years before came back to taunt him.

Freeing himself from the torturing tentacles of his punitive memory, he leveled his gaze calmly at his distraught compatriot, and spoke his mind with settled conviction, "It is the will of God! I must reconcile I am both blessed and burdened with the charge of Noblesse Oblige! So be it!" And then, in an unequivocal tone that struck awe into the heart of Doctor Richards, he remarked coldly and without rancor, "I will meet this man, and he will die! That is the optimal solution! He who plots death unjustly for another, must serve the sentence he himself has imposed. And since his intended victim is the man who gave back our life to me and to the one I love, I surely cannot do less for him. You have done well. I applaud your decision to solicit my assistance."

He paused, thoughtfully, and then continued, "There is one thing I ask: that no one other than you shall ever know the part I have taken in this... and most certainly not Mignonette. She would never understand.

"I shall wear a mask... for reasons obvious to you and me! Make that stipulation clear when you meet with my adversary's second. Give any reason you wish, but be firm on that condition. Extend the same option to him. My procedure is contingent on his acceptance. I believe this war criminal's desire for anonymity is as vital to him as mine is to me.

"I want to settle this matter as quickly as possible. My protracted absence may induce questions in Mignonette's mind, which if asked would elicit a culpable response I wish to avoid. If possible, arrange the duel for no later than tomorrow afternoon, and let me know immediately. I will be here in my room waiting. Go you now, my friend, and God speed! And I must call Mignonette. She will be worried." Doctor Richards nodded, and the two friends embraced and parted.

The following day broke slow but fair... darkness lingers overlong in the shadows of a great mountain. Several miles to the east of Lauzanne a small glade lay in sheltered solitude amidst the decor of a dense Alpine forest. Within its confines a small group of men was deep in serious discussion regarding the conditions relative to the circumstance that had brought them there.

Apart from this group, two men, the active principals involved, each wearing a dark mask, awaited the final disposition of this conversation. One, a large and swarthy individual, eyed his adversary with nervous dissatisfaction, seemingly distrustful of the altered condition that now had removed him from his assumed dictatorial position. The other, taller and more athletically trim, stood in detached contemplation, an attitude of inflexible confidence manifesting in a disdainful smile frozen below his mask, which was perceptively corrosive to the equanimity of his erstwhile antagonist, and further contributed to the man's disconcert.

The official in charge, having familiarized himself with the situation, concluded his initial conversation with the two seconds, and called the contestants to join the group, and explained the rules of combat to be followed. It was standard dueling procedure and took only a moment. "Stand back to back." As ordered, the two men took their positions. "I will count slowly to ten. Take one step on each count... one step only! At the count of ten you will each be free to turn and fire. Your seconds have examined each pistol, and have acknowledged they contain one round only." He handed a gun to each man. "You have six seconds to discharge your weapon after my count of ten. If you fail to do so in that length of time, you may not fire. If you fire your weapon before the count of ten you will automatically draw a charge of murder... and I personally will execute you on the spot. Is that absolutely clear?" Both men nodded in agreement.

The official stepped back and spoke sharply, "Ready?" A pause, "ONE!" The combatants took a step away from one another.

Back at the hospital Doctor Vandermeer had just hung up the phone, where he had been in short but dramatic conversation with Mignonette, who had called to talk to Scott. The circumstances were too plain to be ignored! They both realized Scott intended to take the Doctor's place in that morning's scheduled passage of arms. There was not a moment to waste! His face was ashen, his brain whirling with confused emotion! "Oh! You fool! You glorious fool!" He grabbed a pistol from his desk drawer and rushed out to his car. In a moment he was on the highroad headed for the dueling glade, where he was sure he would find what he sought.

"TWO!" The official's voice rang out like the toll of doom.

Vandermeer's destination was a long five miles away. He mumbled words from a familiar prayer as he sped along, mingled with curses for an implacable fate.

"THREE!" Six paces apart... Seven yet, to the point of doom.

The doctor's knuckles were strained white from the tension of his grip on the steering wheel! "What a noble fool... to risk his life for such as I. Brother... There's a man." The car sped on.

"FOUR!" One more step toward eternity. Six more to doom.

The man at the wheel was praying again. "Dear God! When will it end? We've earned our peace, he and I." Unknowingly he was paraphrasing Kilmeade's thoughts of the night before.

"FIVE!" Somewhere in the branches of a tree nearby, Kilmeade heard the song a bird was singing to its mate... and he thought of Mignonette and their song of the Apple Tree and a silent thought came into his mind... *How wonderful it is to be in love.*

Vandermeer glanced at the odometer: Halfway there! "Oh, the magnificent fool!" But he knew Kilmeade was only doing what he knew he must: "Noblesse oblige."

"SIX!" Time is a strange, a wayward phenomenon. Man does not spend Time... Time expends itself! It's what you do with the opportunity it offers before it is gone that is important! Time waits for no man! Kilmeade knew that awful truth only too well! Five years of his life had slipped away, five vacant and wasted years... never to be reclaimed! His thoughts were calm as he paced into destiny. He swore an oath to himself, "If I live beyond this day, I will make each moment a blessing for my lovely Mignonette and for my precious little son."

Beads of sweat had gathered on Vandermeer's brow as he drew near his destination. "Another mile and I will be there," he told himself. "Just one more mile." He rolled the car window open, the better to hear the sound of gunfire he hoped would not come! Only the whine of the car's motor came to him, and the occasional swish of a branch as his car plunged along. He was deep within the forest now.

"SEVEN!" Kilmeade's adversary wiped the sweat from his gun hand onto his tunic. Just three more paces, if all went well, and he would have his vengeance. He was a man of great violence, and relished the danger of a duel... and the satisfaction of killing his adversary. He had fought three duels, and had come away each time unscathed. Surely this would be a mere repetition of the others. And yet, from the onset it had been different. These silly masks. Why had his opponent insisted that they wear them. Was this man with the dueling pistol in his hand a substitute. Nonsense! He banished the thought from his mind. Whoever he was, he would die like the others. Just three more paces and it would be finished, and he would unmask the man. Anyway, it was too late now for such thoughts. The die was cast. Still... He wiped his hand on his tunic again.

Another hundred yards and Vandermeer would stop the car. He would be there. And then the worst happened! The car staggered and came to a halt. The motor had died... out of petrol. He grabbed his pistol and flung open the door... and lit, running. There's still time... he told himself. There's still time. Not all this for nothing. Dear God... give us just another minute. He thought of Mignonette as he ran. Almighty God... Spare this lovely creature this added grief she cannot survive... and her tiny son, who has known his father for so short a while.

"EIGHT!" Kilmeade looked upward at the sky, and marveled at its beauty.

When this is over, he told himself, I must spend more time with Mignonette, enjoying the wonders of nature that God gave to us. And my precious little son... I will watch him grow to be a stalwart man, and help solve his childhood problems that will seem so big to him.

Back at Marseilles, in the Gulf of Lions, a yacht lay at anchor. In a room below deck, a beautiful woman lay weeping on her bed. A little boy stood beside her speaking comforting words. "Daddy will be all right, Mommy, I know he will. Nothing can take my Daddy from us... You just wait and see." But there were tears in his eyes, too.

Vandermeer could see the open glade now indistinctly through the trees. But something else caught his startled attention.

"NINE!" Kilmeade took a last, deep breath... and with it, the penultimate step, in cadence with the count. The moment of truth was at hand, and he poised himself for the ultimate. He had once questioned the delaying ritual of the duel. But the answer came to him now! It gave advantage to he who was most honorable ... who believed his cause was just! His hand would be the most steady on the final count. Also, it allowed ample time for reconsideration of the validity of the issue involved. He had once witnessed just such an incident: One contestant had, at the count of eight, made apology and admitted he was wrong. When pressed, he had refused to kill or be killed for a trifling pretense.

Then suddenly and insidiously, his thoughts were shattered by the nostalgic thunder of cannon fire from out of the past, muffled by the roar of aircraft overhead. The sky seemed darker for a moment. And then it was gone! But he wondered if it were an omen of his death or an impending travail to again be suffered as a penalty for his courage and address to honor. This, he would not believe, and the structure of his cold-steel nerves retained their unalterable temper... unwavering!

His adversary's gun hand was sweating again, but there wasn't time to wipe it away!

As Vandermeer neared the edge of the clearing he saw a man crouching on his knees holding a rifle fitted with a silencer. With a cry of rage, he impetuously flung himself forward.

"TEN!" Both men whirled simultaneously, and the echo from their pistols blended into one sound! One contestant staggered from the impact of his adversary's bullet, but he did not fall.

His opponent stood motionless for a brief moment, and then sank silently to his knees... a crimson stain appearing over the left breast of his tunic. A moment more he remained thus, a look of incredibility dominating his face beneath his mask. And then he slipped forward to the ground... and death.

Simultaneous with the count of ten, Vandermeer's hurtling body struck the rifleman and bore the man down beneath him, followed by a heavy blow to the man's head with his pistol barrel, knocking him senseless.

As he leaped to his feet, he was aware he had heard gunfire, and he glanced anxiously across the open field where two men stood some twenty yards apart, still confronting each other, their faces hidden behind black masks. Then one sank to his knees, and toppled forward on his face. "Dear God! Which one?" he thought. "I was just in time to save Mignonette. Was I too late to have saved her noble hero?"

He approached, carrying the sniper's rifle, and saw the one man left standing remove his mask. Merciful God, and hallelujah. It was Kilmeade. Vandermeer had again, and indeed been in time.

He rushed to Kilmeade to embrace him, but noticed a red stain on his friend's upper arm. "You're wounded," he said. "I'll have a look at that now, and then to the hospital again for you." He held out the rifle he had taken from the sniper. "They had you set up for an execution. It's good I came when I did. We make a great team." He paused, "But I'm afraid it isn't over yet. You have a lot of explaining to do... Mignonette knows everything." He smiled, "But I'll let you handle that by yourself." They laughed and begged a ride back to the hospital with the dueling official.

The ordeal was over. It all had happened and ended just like one of Scotty's fairy tales.

* * *

Needless to say, Kilmeade and his new bride spent the next two months on an extended honeymoon.

One day, as Scotty's parents lay on deck sunning themselves beneath a cloudless, cerulean sky, the boy emerged from below deck to warn them, "Mommy, Daddy, a storm is coming. Better come inside or you'll get all wet."

"Yes, dear," his mother replied, and dismissed the warning as child's prattle.

"He's right, you know. I'll give it about twenty minutes."

Mignonette gave him an incredulous look! And then exclaimed, as enlightenment overcame her disbelief, "Oh no! Not another one in the family." And then, as a relative thought occurred to her, "Will all our children have your gift?"

"I don't know, dear. But probably just the boys, I think." He smiled, teasing, "We men have to have something you women don't have, you know... to prove our superiority. It's really a women's world, after all." To accentuate his point, he reached and kissed her.

145